December 5, 1987

To dear Ilsa —

I hope you enjoy my _mad_ sense of humor —

Good luck with your work —

Love
Rosemore

The Disenchanted Diva

BY ROSEMARIE SANTINI

The Secret Fire (non-fiction)

Abracadabra

All My Children Books I, II, and III.

A Swell Style of Murder (A Rick & Rosie Mystery)

THE DISENCHANTED DIVA

■

A Rick and Rosie Mystery

■

Rosemarie Santini

St. Martin's Press   New York

THE DISENCHANTED DIVA. Copyright © 1987 by Rosemarie Santini. All rights reserved. Printed in the United States of America. No part of this book may be used or reproduced in any manner whatsoever without written permission except in the case of brief quotations embodied in critical articles or reviews. For information, address St. Martin's Press, 175 Fifth Avenue, New York, N.Y. 10010.

Library of Congress Cataloging-in-Publication Data

Santini, Rosemarie.
   The disenchanted diva.
   I. Title.
PS3569.A546D5   1987   813'.54   87-16388
ISBN 0-312-01020-6

First Edition

10 9 8 7 6 5 4 3 2 1

For Claudia Menza

Una Vera Amica

*I wish to thank my editor,
Toni Lopopolo,
for her support of*
The Disenchanted Diva.

1

It was when Rick Ramsey heard about the cat posse at 950 Park Avenue that he began to take seriously the often quoted biblical prediction that the end of the world would happen in the year 2000 (when he would only be fifty-two). To gear up for this spectacular finish to human consciousness, Rick whispered his favorite mantra, *"Nam Myho Renge Kyo,"* which had been responsible for two jogging buddies getting film deals. His actor pals had sworn that chanting as they trimmed down fat was responsible for Hollywood's recent bid for their talents.

It was 6:30 A.M., Monday, too early to think about success in this life. Instead, Rick was thinking about Aunt Amanda who lived in a nine-room penthouse with her collections. Muses by Matisse. Prints by Picasso. Rare editions. Aunt's late husband, Eric Lord, had served in the United States Senate and had dared to marry Amanda when she was thought quite unmanageable in the eyes of the civilized world. Uncle Eric had taught his wife about the pursuit of money and she had reciprocated by disciplining him in the pursuit of living. After Uncle died of a sudden heart attack, Aunt was unable to personally grant his dying wish to scatter his ashes on a favorite mountaintop located in Afghanistan. The site, unfortunately, was in a state of seige in one of those local wars threatening the peace of the universe. Aunt arranged for the CIA to do it. She still had friends in that agency.

"Nam Myho Renge Kyo."

During this sad year, Rick visited Mandy (his nickname for Aunt) often. At fifty-eight, she was a rare beauty. There were no wrinkles on her face due to her enormous collection of strange creams culled from tiny villages throughout the Third World. This former radical, whose Sunday brunches had set the international scene ablaze with rumor (generally invented by her), had become reclusive. Now, her only companions were Grooms, an aged butler, and two dozen tiger cats.

The cats had gotten Mandy into legal trouble when several strayed out into the halls of her posh art deco building and somehow found their way into the basement. Now, there were several cat dynasties in residence and Mandy's tenants (she owned the building) were threatening a cat posse. The sober residents shuddered at the thought of hordes of cats copulating in the building's lower depths. The elevator was evidence of this and complaints about its feline scents were causing panic in the New York City Health Department.

When Mandy was served with a summons, she'd phoned Rick about the crisis.

"You'll see," she said when he'd arrived at 6 A.M. as requested, "those cats won't leave."

Rick felt his wife, Rosie Caesare, reminded him of Mandy and wondered, since logic and reason did not work on Rosie, would it work on Mandy? He resolved to try.

"Mandy, this situation has cost enormous amounts of your money and time. We've got to get rid of the cats. Uncle Eric would want it this way."

"Sonny, they want to form a cat posse. Imagine! Lynching cats. I thought they stopped that after Caesar lost the Roman Empire. I thought the world was civilized. It's 1988 after all. Time to stop all this anticat nonsense."

"Let's take a look."

Mandy tugged at her elegant burgundy dressing gown. "Alright," she agreed.

In the elevator Rick hummed his mantra because the cat stench was overpowering. By the time they reached the basement, Rick was chanting super loud. When the doors opened, he flashed on his flashlight immediately. The sight was dismaying. The basement was stocked with heavy steamer trunks behind which shiny eyes stared out. Rick wished he had a weapon but Mandy insisted cats were nonviolent.

Slowly, they crept in and out, the torch revealing more and more cat existence.

At the far end of the basement, Rick stumbled.

"What the . . ."

"What is it, Sonny?"

Rick squinted. Punk skinheads had obviously found their way into this cat house because directly ahead were leather belts with bulletheads, shiny sequined masks, several leather whips, leather and silver cuffs for wrists and ankles, and thick heavy chains. This gear was common in SoHo, where Rick lived, but not on upper Park Avenue.

"Mandy, go back upstairs."

"Sonny, I have to free the cats. If I don't, they'll be lynched."

A Wagnerian chorus of meows suddenly filled the basement. A tiger cat with slanted green eyes slinked up to Rick, rubbing his soft fur against Rick's ankles. Rick retreated, having no real fondness for cats. The other cats sensed Rick's dread of felines and grouped. Tails flying high, the group encircled Rick and Mandy. The group got tighter and tighter, until Rick and Mandy could not move without stepping on a cat.

"Poor babies," Mandy whispered. Then suddenly she said, "Sonny, the cats want us to leave."

"How do you know that?"

"Look."

Haughtily, tails high, the cats created a path leading to

the elevator. But Rick's flashlight picked up a strange silhouette behind the cats. Quickly, he snapped the light off.

"Mandy, wait for me in the elevator please."

"Alright, Sonny. Don't be long."

He turned on the flashlight again. *"Nam Myho Renge Kyo,"* Rick chanted loudly hoping this powerful chant would erase the silhouette before him.

"Sonny, are you coming?"

In the elevator Mandy peered at Rick closely.

"Sonny, you don't look very well."

Upstairs, Rick asked Mandy for fresh orange juice, knowing it would take several minutes for her to find Grooms, the aged butler, and several minutes more for Grooms to understand this request. When she disappeared into the maze of rooms, Rick went into the study and dialed the East Fifth Street Police Station.

"Lieutenant Kushel, please."

"Who's this?"

"He knows me."

"What's your name, buddy."

"Rick Ramsey."

"Oh, Rick Ramsey." The cop laughed.

"Yeah, Rick Ramsey. Could I have Lieutenant Kushel, please," Rick asked again.

"You can have anything you want, buddy," the cop said. "Didn't you make a bundle on the Mafia murder?"

Before Rick could answer, he was switched to another extension.

"This is Ryan, find any severed hands lately?"

"Is Lieutenant Kushel there?"

"How about heads? Have you found any heads lying about SoHo?"

"No. But I just found a girl's body. And she's d-e-a-d."

"You kidding?"

"Nope."

Ryan swore.

"Hey, Kushel, that guy, Ramsey, is on the phone. Yeah,

the one who made all that cash on the severed hands book. Yeah. Well, now he says he's found a girl's body. What? I don't know whether she has hands or not. You wanna pick up the phone?"

Kushel's voice sounded grim.

"Ramsey. What is this about?"

"Lieutenant Kushel. I found a dead body in the basement of my aunt's house. It's a girl. She's about seventeen."

"What's the address?"

"Nine-fifty Park Avenue."

"What are you doing up there? I thought you never left SoHo?"

"My aunt lives up here. In the penthouse."

"Is your crazy wife with you?"

"Nope. She's on the movie set."

"That damned movie is driving us nuts. Those guys are in and out of here all the time, interfering with business. They say they got to get authentic stuff. Imagine! The Mayor loves the movies so we don't get paid extra for being nice to those California types."

"Too bad."

"So, who's this body?"

"Don't know."

"What's it look like?" Kushel paused. "You said it has hands. Does it have feet?"

"I think so."

"What do you mean, you think so? Don't you know?"

"Well, it looks pretty grim. I mean, the girl is badly mutilated."

"Mutilated. What do you mean?"

"She has marks all over her body from beatings or something like that."

Rick felt queasy.

"Yeah, what else?" the detective asked without a pause.

"They took her breasts."

"Would you repeat that?"

"She has no breasts."

"No what?" he roared into the phone.

"Her breasts are missing."

"Christ, Ramsey. Can't you ever find a whole body? First it was those severed hands. Now it's severed breasts. What are you going to call this book, *The Severed Breasts*? You're going to make more money and your father-in-law, that crazy Italian dude, is going to bug me to death. Don't touch anything. I'll send a car up right away."

Rick placed the phone back on the receiver when Mandy appeared, carrying a glass of juice.

"Here, Sonny. Freshly squeezed."

"I've got to do a run."

"But Sonny, shouldn't we call the ASPCA about whatever you saw in the basement that upset you so. It was a cat, wasn't it? Was it a dead cat?"

"Mandy, darling, the police are going to be here soon and I'm going for a run. But I'll be back."

"But Sonny . . . what's wrong?"

"I've got to go, Mandy. A Lieutenant Kushel should be with the police."

"Kushel. What kind of a name is that?"

"He's Lithuanian and Rosie's father hates him."

"Achoooo," Mandy sneezed. "What does that Italian have to do with this?"

"Don't think of Mario. You know what Italians do to your allergies."

"Achooo . . . Achooo . . . Achooo," she sneezed.

"I guess I should warn you."

"Warn me about what? Achooo."

"I found the body of a young girl in the basement."

"Oh, Sonny. How horrid of you."

"More horrid for the poor girl."

"Is there anything we can do for her?"

"I'm afraid she's dead, darling."

"Sonny," she stuttered. "Does she have her hands?"

Hands. Hands. Hands. Rick thought he was going to flip. Those severed hands would not leave his consciousness, much as he chanted. His sweet wife was right now doing rewrites on the film based on *The Severed Hands* that they co-wrote. And even before the film, entitled *SoHo Vice* (Hollywood always changed book titles) premiered, he'd found a new body. And this time, the body had no breasts.

"Yes," he answered his aunt's question. "She has both hands. You're not to worry. Lieutenant Kushel will take care of everything when he gets here."

He jogged to the door.

"Where are you going, Sonny?"

"Into another consciousness," he answered.

"I hear it's lovely there! Have a wonderful time," she called as she headed into the living room.

Amanda thought she might be going mad. Policemen in her penthouse? Horrors. The last time she'd spoken to a policeman was during the Paris Riots and only because she'd been arrested. After that time, she'd been able to ignore most of the world's problems, basing her life on the idea of organic symmetry. If events fell into place with the patterned precision of a morality play, then why should she argue with fate and try to change anything.

But why a murder now? And the murder of a poor child?

She sat on the dark tea-rose chaise longue she'd purchased from a Morrocan bordello. Amanda remembered its sensuous history had kept Eric hopping. Smiling, she touched the silk velvet and felt warmed by the memories of happier times.

Life was confusing. Though she was bonded to Eric for most of her adult life, she didn't understand men at all. After she'd fled to Europe and begun her flamboyant rebellion against the strictures of her puritan girlhood, she'd met Eric. Then, he was an oppressive member of the U.S. Senate who told her that all women were created to be wives and that he'd like to set up housekeeping on Park Avenue with her. At first, she refused, but Eric's dark eyes bore right through her wild heart and she submitted. After she began living full-time with a man for the first time in her life, when friends asked her profession, she preferred to say courtesan rather than mannequin.

She'd worked as an aristocratic mannequin in Paris when they met. Her reputation was that she was a gay girl (in those days the word meant fun-loving person), who added an elegance to the social landscape wherever she was. And she was everywhere. London. Paris. Rome. Eric's love resulted in Amanda's dividing her time. Half of her life was spent hidden away with him on Park Avenue; the other half circling the globe.

She was a pioneer of the avant-garde and most of what she and her pals occupied their time with shocked prudish Americans like Eric Lord. They visited nudist colonies in Sweden, caught all the fashion openings in Paris, sat around in Scotland trying to decipher the question of mortality, and attended every party given in Monte Carlo, no matter what season. She seemed most at home in all-night clubs, but would say to Eric that what she really wanted out of life was a nice home. Sanity strained, she would retreat back to their Park Avenue family hearth as a self-renewal movement. Finally, she agreed to marry him. On her wedding day she burst into passionate reveries about the fact that living with a man was a burden. She never changed her mind about that. As time went by, her husband instilled a sense of duty in Amanda which changed all her aristocratic habits. In protest, she ran away from him over two dozen times but she always returned.

"Madame," Grooms's voice broke into her slumbering memories, "the police are here."

Before Amanda stood two young policemen. She viewed their overburdened, clumsy uniforms and thought she could probably design something sensational for the New York City policemen to wear.

"Mrs. Lord," the red-haired, freckled-faced one said to her, "could you tell us what happened?"

"Are you Kushel?" she asked.

"Naw. The detectives will be here later. We got a radio call. Now, could you tell us what happened?"

She glanced at his partner. Of darker skin, his swaggering hips told Amanda he was probably Jamaican.

"I'll tell you what happened, young man," she began, "we were looking for cats. Actually, we were going to round them up to save them from the cat posse when . . ."

"The what?" the dark-skinned policeman interrupted her.

"Don't interrupt me, please," she snapped at him. Then she waved Grooms away to bring coffee immediately. "You see, Sonny, my nephew, was with me. Sonny came to help me with the cats."

"Does this Sonny have a name?" the freckled-face asked.

"Rick Ramsey. Well, you see, we were going through the basement . . ."

"The man who found the handless bodies in the Mafia rooftop murders last year?"

Amanda sneezed, for though the police hadn't mentioned Rosie's name, Amanda's glands reacted as if they had.

"Yes," she said finally. "I believe Rick did discover the Italian hands. Achooo."

"Madame," Grooms added, struggling with the breakfast tray, "may I add that Mr. Rick also discovered the murderer in that caper."

"And wrote a book and got rich," the Jamaican added.

"He was always rich," Amanda corrected.

"Smart guy. Does he go around discovering bodies as a rule?"

"I think this is the first body Sonny has discovered," Amanda insisted. "After all, hands aren't bodies, are they?"

2

Long after many New Yorkers snuggled into bed in their high-rise apartments, another world came to life in the city. At midnight, the young and restless packed into East Village basements. Like Berlin in pre-Nazi times, these clubs were for the disenchanted. Most of the young patrons had spent their teenage years in the city's discos. Now, they arrived nightly, to be part of the scene in places like the Snake Club on East Second Street. The audience consisted of artists, writers, actors. This creative group would dream their dreams during the day, wake up at six P.M. and dress for an evening where they could act out their obsessions. The Snake Club was definitely a place for uninhibited emotions, though it had rules. Dancing was out. So were mild drugs and any kind of straight sex. The in-crowd watched the Snake Club's reviews of sexual experimentation, theme parties celebrating sexual obsessions, art auctions of New Wave paintings, snorted cocaine, and listened to the new music of the future. They set their own fashions with spike wristlets, crew cuts, and multilayered rags. Their rules of conduct stressed passivity so they stared dreamily at the tourists waiting in line who were charged exorbitant cover prices to watch the in-crowd do nothing.

At the Snake Club a young diva called Ice was getting her

one A.M. performance ready by draping herself in purple silk for her act as Little Bo Peep who had lost her sheep. Ice stuffed pillows under her arms and covered her breasts with padded shawls, creating the costume which would transform her into a creature from the world of fabled dreams. Ice's dressing room was a small rear toilet and the closeness of the room affected her badly. In the midst of her preparation, she began gasping. Her face reddened and beads of perspiration formed on her cheeks, melting her thick cake makeup. "Girls Just Want to Have Fun" blasted over the speaker system of the former blue-collar bar. The song was her cue, but Ice was not ready. Peering into the purple-speckled mirror propped against the worn sink, Ice fought panic. A calypso beat joined the recorded music, compliments of Manuelo who, dressed like Carmen Miranda, backed Ice's act with a tin-drum beat.

"I love big juicy cherries," Ice sang as she repaired her makeup.

"Ice Goddess," the crowd screamed.

Ice was a hit on East Second Street.

Suddenly, she stopped working. No more repairs. She would perform as is. Her rouge had run down to her neck. Her mascara had invented drippy fog lines about her eyes, causing a look of melancholy. Her lips were sloppy creamy and she giggled joyfully as she smeared hot red color rub on her cheeks. Well. She was a puppet doll on her way to the trash can where she belonged. Used and worn out. Last year's model. Good only for the trash.

Trashing was Ice's main motif. Each night, she restlessly searched for something new to trash. On the circuit, her uniqueness was that Ice never repeated her act. This earned $50 per performance. It's how she paid her rent. She was a top performer on the mud-club circuit. Many envied her, especially those who were willing to perform for free. But not Ice Goddess. The focus of her performance was slime and trash, mixed with MTV and esoteric elements of Egyptian and cosmic astrology. Fat Man, the Club's owner, asked Ice to add sex to her brash explosion, explaining this would double her salary.

"Men. Women. Kids. Dogs. Cats. Chickens. Sheep. Anything you want, Ice. Anything that turns you on," he said.

Ice became icey.

"Not you, Fat Man," she hissed.

The crowd screamed for her.

"Ice. Ice. Ice. Ice."

They invented her each night.

She went to them.

The club was a dark pit filled with slime and dirt. The previous performer had been a transsexual who performed the two queens, Elizabeth and Mary. As Ice walked to center stage, a sheep ran by and the queen grabbed it. In royal arms, the sheep littered.

The crowd grew hot.

Ice began working the crowd.

"Baby, baby, Bo Peep," she trashed the lullaby and the crowd's early memories.

They laughed.

"Yeah, yeah, yeah," she sang.

She moved close to them and they grabbed her rags. Abruptly she swirled out of reach and the crowd wet their lips in anticipation.

"Beauty," a man yelled above the crowd's roar. "Beauty. Beauty. Beauty."

The crowd laughed at his ardor. He was too passionate. The regulars at the Snake Club insisted that nothing in life was worth anything. Life was to be trashed, along with every emotion.

"Mine. Mine. Mine," he screamed, lunging forward as his punk pals wearing crew hats set out on the throng. Several jumped on tables, their weight crashing the tables, chairs were overturned, people began running from these punks. Some crawled on hands and knees. But one punk grabbed the mike and announced the audience was shit. The crowd yelled as the punks bashed skulls. It was fun and games time on East Second Street. Anguished sounds of pain grew relentless in a celebration chorus. The audience pulled up their arms so spike wristlets would cut the punks. Ice fumbled under her rags until she found her cross. Holding it firmly, she slipped from center stage toward Fat Man's office where a window emptied out onto First Street. It was her escape when the massive skinhead orgies of violence got out of hand. En route to her escape, Ice chanted a prayer.

Violence bored Ice but if she left Second Street she would lose her specialness. She'd begun with New Wave in 1979 when it was forming. Half a dozen years later, New Wave and Ice were swinging into media prominence. Every New Wave pioneer was famous. Painters had launched new art. Rockers had written new sounds. Ice was lucky. She began at twelve and had a rich resume behind her.

Gingerly, Ice hedged bodies as two black belts on Fat Man's payroll bashed skinheads to keep the peace. But the chaos kept swelling into every corner of the cellar. Suddenly, two large arms swept Ice up and carried her out of the club. Under her, people were clawing at each other in the darkness.

"Are you alright, Beauty?" her rescuer asked.

"Yes."

The skinhead wore a red mask and neatly propelled them through the screaming punk mob outside the club. When they reached a parked van, the skinhead placed Ice on the front seat. Through the Leather Man's slits, powerful eyes pierced Ice's frosty coated facade.

3

"Cut."

The director's voice was frosty as he commanded the film crew to stop working. Thankful groans were heard because Stu Vesco had asked for many takes on this rain-soaked morning. The early rain had seeped into the charges to be used to simulate bullets. As a result, nothing happened right. Guns went off out of sequence. Many failed to explode, which caused some performers to lose control. Some were hysterical. Some laughed. Some cried. Most were too tired to protest Vesco's harsh work style. The director kept working nonstop. He sent the special effects people out to clean up the actors and the SoHo street environment. The crew gossiped that Vesco was going to continue shooting without a break, ignoring the Equity ruling for rest periods.

Rosie Caesare, the co-author of the best-selling book, *The Severed Hands*, on which this soon to be released movie, *SoHo Vice*, was based, watched sunlight poking through the heavens. She had written the film's screenplay and knew this scene was supposed to play as a rainy day depression scene. Vesco needed more rain to match his previous shots but, at the same time, the moisture was ruining the special effects. She watched the crew readying an elaborate sprinkler system in the event that God did not cooperate with the director's needs. Rosie knew if the sun grew bright, Vesco would get frantic; so would the producer, Ed Bains. Bains was not a man to be frantic without laying it on everyone in sight, including Rosie.

Actually, she should not be here. Writers were unpopular on the set when performers fed on the lights, the crew's attention, and the camera's observation with the overall motif of the director's dictatorial manner. Because she was a fan of the early Hollywood tradition, when writers, directors and performers were friends, Rosie yearned for that sense of comradery. Nowadays, directors and actors competed with writers. The eighties' cutthroat competition was the reason that Rosie wrote mostly books and lived in SoHo, instead of renting a place at Malibu that her husband, Rick Ramsey, said they could now afford but added, he wouldn't be caught dead there.

A native of SoHo, Rosie loved West Broadway, the locale the movie company was using today. But she was on guard because a member of her nearby family might drop by and accuse her of betraying her clan. Her best-selling book was about a Mafia murder which had taken place on a SoHo rooftop. The Caesare clan felt that it dragged the Italian people through the mud. Her father, Mario, wasn't speaking to her and her mother, Celia, made angry, guttural noises whenever Rosie phoned. They were speaking to Rick, though, because her husband and co-author wasn't Italian and thus wasn't bound by the same set of rules that held Rosie prisoner.

Rosie didn't mind about her various uncles, aunts, cousins, and second cousins, because there were too many of them to speak to and remain sane. And she was used to her mother being angry at her. But her Dad's anger hurt. Mario had been against the book even though he understood that she and Rick were writers and had to tell the truth. When Hollywood took an option on the book, Mario had insisted things had gone too far.

"It'll show all over the world. Everyone will think we live in the gutter. Is this what you want?" he shouted.

"No, Dad."

"Why don't you write something about Leonardo da Vinci? Eh? How about Christopher Columbus? He was Italian. We can be proud of those guys."

"They won't sell."

"Money? Is that all there is to life?"

"You're not Mafia. Neither is anyone in our family. So why do you care?"

"I care."

Mario's cherub face turned pink and tears began to form in his eyes. Rosie was always respectful of the natural acting ability of anyone with Italian blood. Without training, he and most Italians could cry, laugh, sing and dance at will. They loved the movies and though most of SoHo's Italians had not read her book, she knew once it became a movie, every resident of every house on every SoHo block would attend.

"Isn't your life more important than success?" her father asked.

"The Mafia is worried about the Pizza Connection. They're not going to notice the book."

"And what about you and Rick? Eh? Has your career become more important than your marriage? Your happiness?"

As usual, Mario socked it to her right in the gut. While success was terribly important to Rosie, so was Rick. They'd been married for six years and were co-authors of a bestseller. They lived in a lovely SoHo loft and with their royalties were thinking of buying a villa near Florence because Mario loved that city and Rick and Rosie thought they would, too.

So why was she working so hard?

She knew it wasn't for the money. Not only was Rick's trust fund large enough for them to afford a SoHo life-style, but the profits of their best-seller had bought extras like a jeep with pink calico seats. Aside from a few frivolities and tax shelters, their life hadn't changed. They still lived in SoHo where they strolled the streets, hand in hand, and they were still deeply in love.

Then Hollywood beckoned. Rick hated the West Coast and he had absolutely refused to co-write the screenplay with Rosie, even though she promised he'd never have to leave SoHo. His decision had caused a severe jolt in her trust. Now she felt confused. Hadn't they said they would always write together? What does a thirty-four-year-old woman do when she's worked all her life for success, and when she gets it, she finds out it costs too much?

Her mother had an answer.

"It's time for you to get pregnant."

Rosie wasn't about to get pregnant but she couldn't lose Rick. He was her best friend, her husband, her lover. And he'd been right about film people. After two months, she hated their inflated egos, the long waits between shots, the constant rewrites, the drugs. In the film world, everyone seemed to have an image to protect and lived surrounded by flunkies. It was a very fragile life. She wanted out before she became one of them.

"Damn."

Ed Bains put his arm around Rosie's shoulder, his manicured fingertips edging down towards the tips of her full breasts. Gracefully, she shrugged his arm from her body. When was Bains going to realize that she was a writer, not a media toy?

Bains shrugged. Then he put his other arm around her.

"Vesco needs more rain. If he doesn't get it, we're in the dump."

Again, she moved away from his touch. Sourly, he stared at her, behind large dark glasses that helped him never age. A man subject to great mood swings, Bains would be absolutely frantic over his financial situation one minute, and the next, the market would take an upward swing and change his mood. He lived like a character in a Sidney Sheldon novel, with houses in every major city and a private plane fitted with relaxation equipment. But, when he was in trouble, Bains acted like the grandson of the Lebanese immigrant that he was. But, his behavior was a farce, for he was like most other third-generation Harvard-educated producers. Their fathers had been the sons of hardworking immigrants who had talked about good pictures and building stars. But their grandsons talked only about computer printouts of profit and loss.

Nowadays, every form of art was controlled by computer printouts.

Rosie could handle that. But Rick couldn't.

"Hey, Rosie Caesare," a grip on the set shouted.

"Yes, I'm here."

"Your husband said he has to talk to you right away."

"Is he okay?"

"He sounded flippy."

"Flippy?"

"Yeah, is he into coke or something?"

"Rick doesn't do drugs."

"Well, he must be on something. He told me to tell you that he found another body and this time there were no breasts."

4

"*I hear,*" Miles Hamilton said from his London suite, "that you've found another body and this one has no breasts."

"Good news travels fast," Rick quipped. Since he'd found the poor girl's body, he'd been in a state of suspense. As usual, this state produced strange physical reactions.

All through the grilling at Mandy's Rick had noticed that he was erect. Though he'd documented during his last bout with crime and the Mafia, that overt fear produced constant erection, he hadn't realized that hostility could do it, too. During the infamous severed hands affair, he'd been making love to his adorable Rosie often. But these days, he was not. This caused terrible frustration but Rick vowed to handle it. After all, he was a human being, not an animal. And, as Rosie was fond of reminding him, they were both free souls mating in this present incarnation of their existence. Rick felt they had been man and wife in other lives, for theirs was a special closeness, an intimacy, which could not have been simply created in the brief years of their relationship. Because of this closeness, Rick would not have a go at another woman.

But there was another reason, too. Rosie would probably kill him.

She'd explained more than once that Italians do not believe in divorce (though current statistics would disprove this) and that murder was their answer in cases of infidelity. Though Rosie laughed when she said this, Rick wasn't sure whether she was joking.

How odd that they were suited to each other. Rosie, with her passionate Italian SoHo background, and he, from his bland wealthy New England life. Rick felt his New England background had made him too rigid about life, love, and the pursuit of happiness. He'd lived in Connecticut until he was fourteen, emigrating with his family to SoHo for a complete change of consciousness regarding life. Rick's memories of that New England life were still very vivid.

People lived differently there. Privacy was their only passion. His family, the Ramseys, roped off land like most of the Old Guard, posting notices which read VISITORS NOT WELCOME. His hometown was on the water and in summer, small yachts and boats crammed the harbor. Everyone sailed. Rick's father would sit in a glass-enclosed porch watching over their carefully manicured lawns as the rest of the family manned their boat.

Rick's father was a major in the U.S. Army. At home, he always dressed with casual graciousness. Sports jacket in a subdued plaid. A natty blue and white striped shirt. Patterned tie. Buckled loafers. All the men in town were like the very proper Major Ramsey. Rick spent most of his childhood wondering if he were the only person who had wet fantasies. Did sex exist in Connecticut? When he moved to SoHo, Rick learned that sex existed everywhere. Rosie and her Italian family had a mystical view of sex, which Rick couldn't quite fathom, although it earned his admiration. Mario explained that everyone fussed over sex too much. After all, sex was a completely natural act. Sometimes one wanted sex and sometimes one didn't.

Rick found that ever since he met Rosie, he always wanted sex. (She was fourteen and he was sixteen at the time.) His appetite for her lush body never let up. Rosie was gorgeously sensuous. Later, when they became lovers, a door opened into his life that his New England background had not prepared him for. In Connecticut, one never spoke above a polite murmur. When he met Rosie, Rick was shocked at the fact that Rosie and the rest of her family spoke with verve and vigor, at all times. Especially, he liked the sounds Rosie made when he made love to her. He loved the way she gasped when he touched her, the way her long legs circled his waist as he explored her, his flesh with her flesh, wet and hot. He loved reaching the final round (Rosie's term for orgasm). His earth-oriented wife would explain that orgasms were good for the circulation of the blood. Rick liked orgasms because he reached a plateau of mystical ecstasy he'd often read about in those strange books with old leather covers. Loving Rosie was pure joy, an experience Rick hadn't known until he met her.

But that was before success and Hollywood had beckoned for his lady's attention.

"Nam Myho Renge Kyo."

Rick chanted, shrugging away all negative vibes from his consciousness. He vowed to be the warm, loving husband Rosie needed. He would concentrate on understanding his wife's psyche. He'd hurt her in the past and never wanted to repeat his ungallant behavior in any shape or form. If Rosie didn't presently desire sex, he'd stand by her faithfully. But his damn body wasn't helping, because all he could think of was sex with Rosie. That's what happened when a sensitive virile boy grew up in a place where sex was denied, instead of in the midst of an Italian family where sex was everywhere to be acted upon when a person was old enough to handle its passion.

"Rick. Ricky, are you there? Do we have a bad connection?" Miles rasped, bringing Rick's thoughts from sex to murder.

"Let's not talk about the murder, please," Rick pleaded.

"Sweetheart, Rosie and you have another best-seller on your hands. Imagine what good luck, your finding that body. It's as good as the first time, I mean, when you found the hands."

"Miles, it's not the same."

"Get on this case, Rick. I talked to Rosie and she agreed that this would be a dynamic second book."

"How did you find Rosie?"

"She called me from the set, of course. Come on, Rick. Start working. Rosie says you need something to occupy yourself. She says you've been mooning around the house ever since *SoHo Vice* has been on location."

Rick was mooning around the house because he was lonely for his beloved. But he couldn't confess this to Miles because Rosie liked to keep their personal life private.

"Miles, I don't think I want to do another murder book. I'm tired of violence. I want peace and quiet."

"At thirty-six?" Miles screamed. "You'll be b-o-r-e-d, and so will R-o-s-i-e," he spelled. "Besides, you could always use another mil."

"I'm not interested in money."

"But your darling mate is. Thank God, women are pragmatic or men would go straight down the tubes. My darling mother keeps me on the straight and narrow. Whenever I want to turn in my agent's job and go to the Islands for sweaty bodies and lime juice, Mom says, 'Miles, remember how poor we were? Well, we're rich and it's better.' Ricky, she's absolutely right."

"But I've always had money."

"Being born to puritan money is not the same as getting it straight from Hollywood. *Comprende?*"

"*Si, si.* But I don't like it."

"Hey, what's wrong, fella?"

Miles was suddenly compassionate.

"My life is a mess. Rosie is never home."

"I suppose the next thing you're going to hit me with is that Rosie doesn't cook anymore. You're liberated, for heaven's sake, hire a cook."

"It's not food I'm missing."

"Oh, I see."

Miles retreated. He was a Southern man who believed

that personal sex should reside in that realm of mystical eroticism which Southern writers were great at recording for the rest of the world.

"Ricky," he said, "this is a God-sent opportunity for another best-seller. You simply can't turn it down. For Pete's sake, the girl was seventeen years old, wasn't she? Don't you want to find out who her murderer is?"

"How do you know she's seventeen years old?"

"Rosie told me."

"How does she know?"

"She's a good reporter, that's how."

"Miles, I don't want to put in another year like the last one."

"What's so bad about the last year? Bulloghs published your book and you made a paperback sale in six figures. And Collier Films, Limited optioned you and then went ahead with the film. Am I wrong or did I forget something?"

"Look, do you know what it was like, finding severed hands everytime I went out? Do you think it was great being threatened by the local Mafia? If it wasn't for Mario, I'd probably be dead."

"Don't be dreary, Rick," Miles countered. "Remember, in the final analysis, it wasn't the Mafia who killed those people without hands."

"It was a weirdo."

"And you're simply marvelous with weirdos. Now, we know it must be a weirdo who killed that poor young child and mutilated her breasts."

"How did you . . ."

"Rosie." Miles paused. "Ricky, you must do this book. It's important. You simply cannot be selfish."

"Miles, I don't think so."

Miles was impatient again.

"Talk to Rosie before you decide," he said. "Good-bye."

Rick knew that he would lose the battle because Rosie was obviously hot on this new project. Whenever Rosie was hot for something, she pursued it with the persistence of a Roman army, which was where she learned her strategy.

Rosie explained that she was impatient for success because she'd spent eight long years mourning for Rick. When Rick thought about that sad time in their lives, he always felt guilty. During that time, Rosie had written books filled with bitterness and regret, but the public wasn't having these true tales of women's suffering so the books bombed.

After they married, Rosie explained her life without Rick in one word.

"Grief."

"I thought you were jealous."

"No, it was pure and simple grief."

There was good reason and it was all his fault. After getting engaged at Rosie's high school prom, and then, scandalizing the entire Caesare clan by running off to live in sin, inexplicably, Rick eloped with tall, unruffled Sharon Neiman two years later, leaving his beloved to fend for herself in the world of loneliness, family alienation, book publishers, and men. Just recently, Rick realized that he had fled from Rosie because he loved her too much. He was afraid of the deep intimacy, the almost-too-personal closeness Rosie demanded. His WASP blood hadn't prepared him for her intense Italian passion, He simply wasn't ready for that kind of committed life. But after living with Sharon, who avoided all possibility of caring by an endless round of parties and cocaine, Rick decided that he'd rather take his chances living with Rosie. Happily, Rosie took him back with open arms.

"Why was it grief and not jealousy?" Rick asked, when they could talk about that time.

"When you married that tall twit I thought my life was over. Mario vowed to kill you, but I'm nonviolent."

"Your father wanted to kill me? I thought he liked me."

"Didn't you deserve it?" Rosie asked with incredulously innocent eyes.

"What happened?"

"Obviously nothing, you're still here, aren't you?"

Her eyes shone with revenge.

"For eight years, I stayed home and cried for you. I ran around the apartment grabbing up all your things. I tried to torch them but when I saw your cashmere socks, the ones we bought in Maine, well, I couldn't do it. So I put all your things in storage and thought, when Rick comes back, he'll have something to wear."

"Baby, can we forget about it?"

"I kept looking for you, Rick. In bed. At breakfast. You were part of my life and there I was, all alone. That's when I realized that grief for a man can make a woman crazy."

Her emerald eyes gazed at him until he shuddered.

"I'm sorry."

"Sorry isn't good enough. When the eight years were over and you came back and we got married, I made a promise to myself that I would never devote myself to anyone again."

"I love you, Rosie."

She softened, leaned over and kissed the tips of his lips, his nose, his cheeks, his eyes. At her touch, he ignited and looked deep into her eyes.

"Rosie," he whispered. "I promise. I'll never leave you."

5

"*The thing is*, darling..." Rosie said, wrapping herself in a soft pink bath towel, her dripping hair causing tiny bubbles of beautiful stars to frame her Rubens face, "we must do this new book. I think it'll be very important for us."

As she unclasped the towel from her body, she swiveled about, hips and shoulders unconsciously moving into a graceful rhythm.

"After all, kids are important. Dad always says kids are the world's conscience."

"He's right," Rick agreed.

"Dad says that whatever our sins are, we can look at our kids and see the results. That's why he's always fretting about you and me, Rick."

"I'm not his son."

"You practically are."

Smiling, Rosie did a quick turn on her toes and stepped into a pair of pink panties with red hearts embroidered on them. They were trimmed with Irish lace and were a heavy duty gift from Aunt Irene, Mario's rich sister-in-law and their landlord. Rosie snapped on a matching bra, causing her breasts to swell into an upward bobbing motion. Then, quickly she touched her breasts.

Rick watched her. Rosie had been checking out her breasts ever since he found the corpse in Mandy's basement. Smiling at his wife, Rick opened his arms wide to comfort her.

Sometimes it must be hell being a woman, he thought. They were so mysterious. He'd known Rosie for twenty years. Except for his leave of absence when he was married to Sharon, he saw Rosie practically every day. And still, her persona was muted in mystery. He understood some things about her, but there were other traits and beliefs that were still unfolding.

He kissed her forehead and held her close. This mystery made Rosie exciting to live with. Every day was another adventure.

"Have you heard from Dad?" she asked softly.

"I'm seeing him tomorrow. I think he's ready to make up."

She looked sad.

"I hope so. He's never been mad at me for such a long time."

"Your father adores you," Rick whispered. "I adore you, too."

"Thanks, darling," she said, quietly pecking his cheek.

Though their loft was quite large, Rosie's sense of design had created several areas of intimacy. In the large living space, a sparkling white grand piano dominated the entrance off the elevator. Further to the left, in front of a wall of tall windows, two soft plum Victorian couches formed a seating space. Because the couches reminded Rosie of Bloomsbury, one of her favorite literary eras, she was fond of calling the sitting area Woolfe's lair. Cane-back *Casablanca* (Rosie's favorite film) chairs added diversity to Woolfe's Lair, and so did the used Persian rug of dark blue background and tea-rose design.

Though their bedroom at the end of the loft was large and filled with several closets, Rosie's huge wardrobe of fun disguises and serious business outfits required more space. So, there were several wall-to-wall closets bordering Woolfe's Lair. Now, she danced over to one.

"I don't know what to wear to that meeting with Bains. He's a macho pig and everything I wear turns him on."

"You turn him on."

"I wish I didn't, though I'm sure it's not personal. It's simply the fact that I am a member of the female sex."

"You certainly are."

She laughed.

"He wants me to rewrite the last scene again. Why do I have to meet him? Does he want to sharpen my pencils?"

"You tell me if he touches your pencils."

She laughed again.

"His assistant called and said, 'Mrs. Ramsey.' Of course, I corrected him and told him my name was Ms. Caesare, but the cutie pie went right on without a second breath and said, 'Mrs. Ramsey, Mr. Bains will expect you at the Odeon Restaurant at four P.M.' Rick, sometimes I think men who end up as secretaries hate women."

"I don't blame them."

Quickly, she glanced at Rick, trying to identify his response with what she'd said. Then, shaking her head, she continued searching through the closet, moving briskly so wet sprints from her hair sprinkled Rick.

"Hey, that's cold," he complained.

"Feeling hostile, darling?"

"How would you feel if you hadn't had sex for three weeks?"

"I haven't had sex for three weeks, either, remember? I'm your partner. Your own true love. So, if you haven't, I haven't."

"But it's your choice, not mine."

"It's not my choice, it's simply a necessity. You know about Freud's libido theory, don't you?"

"Fuck Freud. He's made it hard for the rest of us."

Concerned, she examined the expression on his face, then

walked back to the couch where she sat next to Rick and put her arms around him.

"Don't stop now," he said.

"Rick, I'll be late."

"Be late."

But she skipped away again, paused, then selected a jade green silk dress that Rick loved. He thought Rosie looked like a ninth-century Chinese goddess when she wore it.

"The way I see it, Rick," she said, "we've got a kiddie culture going. And our book can investigate it."

"What's a kiddie culture?"

"Uh, huh," she murmured, stooping to pile her hair way up on the top of her head, then fastening her locks into an arrangement of tiny spit curls, she topped the crown of curls with one of the tea roses Rick had brought home last night. She'd been happy about the flowers but his romantic notions hadn't swayed her.

"Rosie . . ."

"Rick, I want to make love to you. In fact, I'm dying to make love."

Rick sprung to his feet, already out of his jogging shorts.

"No, sweetheart. I can't. I've got to be at the Odeon at four. You know how Bains hates anyone to be late."

"Fuck Bains."

"More hostility."

"What do you expect?"

Softly, she said, "Rick, it's not going to be for too much longer. I'll be finished with the picture at the end of this week."

"You were finished with the picture the day you cashed the check. Miles says you don't have to rewrite. They can get somebody else to do that."

"Miles doesn't understand that I'm a perfectionist. Besides, Collier Films has been good to us."

"Fuck Collier Films."

"That again."

Slowly, she walked toward Rick, hands on her hips, shaking her head.

"Fuck everyone, is that it?"

"Yes, because I can't have you."

"You can. In a few days they're wrapping up the location and then they're off to Hollywood."

"I don't want you to go there."

Furious at his tone, she answered angrily.

"I have no intention of going. Rick, please, don't tell me what to do. I don't tell you what to do, do I?"

"No, but you make it impossible for me to do what I want to do."

"What's that, darling?"

"Make love."

Furtively, she kissed him.

"I'll be home early and we'll have a whole evening to ourselves," then said to herself, "Oh, what am I doing? I promised myself I wouldn't."

"Wouldn't what?"

"Cater to your romantic needs."

"What's wrong with catering to my physical needs?" he insisted. "You know, my blood hasn't been circulating lately."

Her eyes moistened.

"Darling . . ."

"This is a two-way street, Rosie. Remember that. A liberated marriage has two pathways. I understand your needs and your psyche. But you must understand mine."

"You're right, Ricky. I'm sorry."

She sat on his lap and kissed him.

"Sometimes I forget," she whispered into his ear. "But you're patient and wonderful."

"Sometimes you forget what?"

"That loving is sharing."

Rick put his arms around her.

"That's why I'm here."

"Why?"

"To remind you."

Passionately they kissed. Then they rolled over, falling onto the Persian rug.

"It's itchy," she complained.

"What is?"

"The rug."

"Lie still, baby. There's something I want to say."

"Yes, I do, too."

"Do what?" Rick asked.

"Love you."

Tightly he held her to him, listening for heartbeats. She moved, kissing him, traveling to his toes, then up again, his ankles, calves, knees, covering his body with wet kisses. Each time her lips touched his flesh, Rick caught fire.

"Lie back," she cooed. "I want to make up for these awful weeks."

"No guilts," Rick reminded her.

"No guilts," she agreed.

Rick held Rosie close, his arms entwined around her loveliness, breathing in her fragrance, feeling the wonder of her. Rosie was the center of his life, the core of his strength. For all her eccentricity, her battles with liberation and selfishness, her theories on the new marriage, her compulsive workaholic ways, his wife loved him warmly and he felt very lucky.

"I couldn't live without you," he said.

"I wouldn't want to live without you," she moaned.

Always Rosie opened her heart and body to him, not withholding anything, in a trusting way which mystified Rick. She possessed a strange primitive sense that she could trust Rick to enter her body where he would please her and never hurt her. Because of her trust, Rick always tried his very best to do just that.

It was a while before Rosie remembered to call Bains's office. When she phoned, she explained that she had an accident in a taxi and had to go to the hospital to check out whether her nose was broken.

When she hung up, Rick laughed.

"Couldn't you simply say you had cramps?"

"I never use women excuses."

Rick hugged her.

"My brave gladiator lady. No, you don't, do you?"

"Darling, you know the real reason I love you is that you're beyond sex."

"Not too beyond, I hope."

"I mean it. You really love me, Rick. For a woman, that's important to know."

"I'm glad to know it," Rick said. "Here, let me show you again."

Afterwards, she became serious. "I want to swing right into this project as soon as the film is wrapped."

"The film won't be wrapped for weeks."

"I mean the SoHo part." Gleefully, she laughed. "There's one good reason to write the new book, Rick. A book makes me normal."

He laughed.

"You're never normal, darling."

"When we write together, we're together."

"I see. Blackmail."

"Hollywood makes me crazy, Rick. I don't know why."

"It makes us all crazy."

"Look at what it's done to kids. Everybody wants to be one of those goons in the MTV videos. All that sadomasochism the kids watch, as if it was normal. Maybe that's how that girl got mutilated. Poor girl. Dying without breasts."

She shook her head sadly, then nervously touched her heaving chest. Rick took her hands and kissed them.

"The Major told me that sadomasochism with very young girls is common in South America. He used to tell me stories about his travels there when he was with the army."

"Ugh. Your father was weird."

"Mother would never listen. She'd disappear as soon as he began one of his tales."

Rick pointed to the magazine rack nearby.

"I thought it only happened in South America. But look at all this."

He picked up several news magazines. On every cover was a child or sex abuse story.

"Rick, you do care."

"Mario is right. Sex is great, but not when it's used on little kids."

"Dad always hated kids being used for anything by the media. When I was four, a photographer saw me in Washington Square Park and asked Dad if he could use me as a model. Dad said no, she's only a child."

"Good for him."

"I wonder what would have happened if I'd been exposed to that kind of life. Hollywood would have been harder to resist, I think."

Rosie bit her lower lip, a gesture held over from her teenage years. Rick remembered the first time he'd seen her do that. Was that the moment when he fell in love with her? He didn't know. He remembered many moments. He held her tightly and kissed the tip of her nose.

"I've seen some of those kids," she continued. "On the set, they're treated like pieces of meat, surrounded by agents, gofers, and greedy mothers. We have two on *SoHo Vice*. One has freckles and melts your heart. The other has gorgeous blue eyes. When they're alone, they wisecrack in a sophisticated way. They've got pimples, growing pains, and things other kids have, but they're not allowed to be kids."

She paused for a second, her eyes glowing.

"You wonder whether they were ever kids. Their mothers hang around and tell them they have to do everything the director tells them. They're taught to please everyone. They develop a thick skin and will do anything to avoid rejection or criticism. After that, it's easy to train them to obey sexual commands."

"How do you mean?"

"They're not taught to be discriminating. When I was growing up, Dad told me never to be alone with a man. Not an uncle. Not a doctor. Not even a priest. I didn't understand why. Then, when I was twelve, there was a scandal in SoHo. A priest abused a young girl. I understood immediately what Dad meant. So you see, he taught me early that I could disobey people in authority. That's why I'm a rebel."

"Hard to live with, but wonderful to love."

She blew him a kiss.

"Thanks."

"Little boys go through this, too. In Connecticut, where nobody ever heard of sex, there were rumors that boys who were sent to British private schools had terrible experiences."

"All the research I've looked at says that pedophiles really think they're giving little kids love."

"Hey, when did you have time to do research?"

"We're rich, so I hired a research team."

She jumped up, her bare buttocks waving adorably. Rick watched her, thinking that he was blessed to have a wife with an exciting body and a mind to match. Though Rosie had strange quirks, he was never bored.

"Here," she said, handing him a thick folder.

He measured the thickness of the file.

"Well, this will keep me busy for a while."

"Please, Rick. Think seriously about it."

"You really want to do this, darling?"

"We have to."

"You realize that we're going to have to deal with all sorts of awful things."

"We're investigative reporters, aren't we?"

"My brave girl."

"Woman."

"My brave woman."

"Besides, we can do a best-seller which means lots of people will read about this awful stuff. We may save some kids. Parents will be more careful. You see?"

"But we're not really sure yet that this is a child molestation case."

"I am."

She pulled out an envelope. Reaching into it, she produced a photograph of the girl's corpse. Rick concentrated on not getting sick, whispering his chant as he examined the photo with its police markings.

"How did you get this?"

"From one of our contacts at the police department. Horrible, isn't it?"

"Poor kid."

Rick stared at the photograph, wondering how the teenager had become the victim of the freaks. Did she do it for the money? Did she do it because she was frightened? Were they holding her captive?

Suddenly, he thought, could it have possibly been because she liked it?

6

"*Hey, kid,* what is it with you anyway?"

Mario Caesare's cherub lips chomped down on the Cuban cigar he wasn't supposed to be smoking.

"Last year, it was the hands. This year, it's a body with no breasts. Are you doing this on purpose?"

Trying to be solemn, Rick looked at Mario. They were standing at the corner of Prince Street and West Broadway, where Collier Films Ltd. was reproducing a hardware store. The former store was now the Neon Boutique and the set designers were working hard to restore a look of sturdiness that the store had had only last year. Hollywood set designers were good at manufacturing reality locations, to the tune of billions of dollars. Location shooting was cheaper in New York City because the Mayor gave the police to the film company, free of charge. The blue uniforms felt privileged to be part of the film and did whatever the director asked them to do.

Rick watched the film company's rented trucks line the street. Some were white with pink-striped awnings. Others were blue with yellow stars. The air conditioning was operating full blast, though it was not a hot day. A catering truck stood by offering several course meals, served al fresco to the crew and performers. Several SoHo residents who looked Italian were assumed to be extras and were stuffing themselves. Everything illustrated that this was an Italian movie, for the pasta was prepared al dente and the veal was thinly sliced.

The performers, too, conveyed an Italian flavor. The men were sturdy, dark haired, and unshaven. The women were dressed in peasant skirts and blouses, ready to reproduce a flashback sequence. All had long braids worn in a high crown on top of their heads.

When Rick first lived in SoHo as a teenager, he'd lived in fear. Then he learned that the local Italians were gentle and respectful although they viewed life as a constant source of danger. As a result, they were very secretive. Many men hung out at a private club and though, they were not necessarily "connected" (a term meaning to be part of the Mafia) they pretended they might be. Even Mario lunched there from time to time, to touch base, though Mario hated all beasts (Rosie's name for gangsters). But Mario knew he must live and let live, especially when one lived in SoHo.

"Hey, let's sit here," Mario gestured to a table at a corner cafe.

Rick noticed the older man seemed tired.

"Are you alright?"

"You bet your ass," Mario announced, pushing the cigar stump into a glass ashtray. The cigar was too large and particles careened over the table. Immediately, Mario clapped his hands and a waitress in a short, black skirt appeared.

"Please clean this up," Mario asked brusquely.

As she wiped off the table, Mario looked at the girl's orange stockings, her torn T-shirt top, her frizzy orange/red hair and shook his head, conveying his compassion for most of humanity. When the waitress swept some of the cigar litter onto his Giorgio Armani suit (Mario was always conscious of the *bella figura*—making the best impression), he grimaced, jumped up from his chair, shook off the debris and sat down again.

Though Mario gave the impression of great strength, he

actually was rather slim. Only his massive chest revealed hints of hard work on the waterfront when he was a young boy. His sturdiness encased in natty suits he had tailored for him in Florence gave him the look of a Renaissance sculptor, a look which fused extreme intelligence and sensitivity of thought with the brutal physical strength necessary for work in stone quarries.

Suddenly, Mario's shoulders slumped with the wisdom of his fifty-plus years.

"These young girls. They're not like anybody I've ever known. They walk around, all body, but no sense." He pointed to his forehead. "Thank God, my Rosie isn't that way. She's smart." Then, "Look, Rick. My daughter's future is in your hands. I'm not going to live forever."

"Hey, Mario. Are you sure you're feeling okay?"

"Naw, it's nothing. My doctor says I gotta slow down a little, that's all. But how can I slow down? Being alive means there's lots to do, no? That's why I want to talk to you about Rosie."

"I love her."

"Don't be an idiot," Mario scolded. "Of course, you love her. But what's more important, are you going to drag up a murder every ten months and ruin her life?"

Watching Mario, Rick wondered how Italians kept up their healthy robust complexions in pallid, fumy Manhattan.

Rick worked hard to look healthy. Daily, he went to Mallory's Health Club to work out. He jogged on SoHo streets at every opportunity (that's how he'd discovered the severed hand). Willingly, he dined on whatever Rosie's latest lettuce leaf fetish was. As a result he was strong and slim and often was compared to television's Magnum, though he knew Tom Selleck's eyes were dark brown and his own were what Rosie called true blue.

"I'm willing to forget about this murder," Rick said evenly. "In fact, I'm willing to forget about any murder."

"Then why did you discover a body, for God's sake?"

"Mario, it wasn't my fault. I was helping Aunt Mandy

get rid of her cats. And there was this body. Was I supposed to leave it there?"

"You left the hands when you found them. Remember? That was smart. But then you went back to being stupid. You almost went to jail."

Rick didn't want to remember the *hands* caper.

"Then, I was stupid. Now I know better. Besides, Kushel and the New York City Police Department watch over us."

Predictably, Mario grew indignant at the mention of police surveillance. His bright eyes narrowed in an Oriental slant, their green shade glowing maliciously while his cherub lips tightened in a George Raft smile.

"Has that Lithuanian detective been bothering you?" he demanded.

"*Kiss of Death*, 1947 or 1948, starring Richard Widmark and Victor Mature."

"Stop that," Mario scolded, knowing Rick was a film nut who often used movies to describe life.

Mario snapped his fingers at the orange-haired waitress.

"Espresso. Rick?"

"Earl Grey Tea."

At the mention of the tea, Mario grimaced. Then he waved away the waitress to her task.

"So, I asked, the police been bothering you?"

"Kushel hasn't. But I think there are cops on the set."

"Yeah, those cops love the Mafia," Mario laughed gustily. "Besides, they'll do anything to be in a movie."

Two actresses began taking down their braids, frizzing out their hair to look normal for their journey on the New York subway system. Petite, almost anorectic, their bright eyes were defiant. Suddenly, one spotted Rick and walked over to the table.

"Are you the author of this trash?"

"Nope."

The actress looked blank, then shrugged her shoulders and walked away.

"I guess we didn't pass the test. I don't know why. I read Shakespeare, Shaw, Pinter, and Ionesco," Rick quipped.

"But not Dante," Mario retorted with contempt.

"I'll try him again," Rick promised.

"My daughter read Dante when she was ten. By the time she was fourteen—around the time she met you—she'd read Machiavelli."

"It shows," Rick responded mischievously.

A few doorways down the street, Rick saw the director, Vesco, signal that he was ready to shoot.

"Action," Vesco shouted.

Several groups of Italian passersby watched noisily. Vesco sent assistants to quiet them. Sounds of dissatisfaction grew louder and the police joined the crowd. Mario smiled.

"What's happening?" Rick asked.

Mario's face contained the expression of a Cheshire cat, an expression Rick knew intimately because Rosie was fond of using it.

The crowd continued to protest, marching with hands intertwined, chanting, "Leonardo da Vinci. Christopher Columbus."

"What's that about?"

"They're calling out our Italian geniuses."

Rick noticed there were no women in the crowd and surmised this demonstration had been planned because Italians never sent women into violent situations.

"Are you behind this?"

Mario laughed.

"Sure. Americans forget that we Italians are great geniuses. All they think is Mafia."

"Come on, Mario. Americans think Italians are sexy and wonderful and fun."

"You want to bet? We're treated like lepers. No one trusts us. That's why we're loyal and secretive and stick together like glue."

"That's silly."

"Rick," Mario shouted, "when are you going to accept reality?"

"Mario. My family always visited Rome."

"Hey, get off my back," Mario retorted angrily. "Your family was crazy. I remember how the Major collected dirty cans from the streets to make his sculptures. Imagine? A retired U.S. Army man kneeling in the gutter for raw materials? In Italy, our sculptors go to the quarries. They use the best marble. Look at the statues in the squares, in the churches. *Magnifico!*"

He kissed the tips of his fingers dramatically.

"Not this SoHo art. This is junk!" Mario declared for posterity.

Before Rick could answer, the waitress appeared, carrying a tray. Carefully, Mario watched her, suspecting that she was a druggie and could drop anything. When she managed to serve the hot refreshments without causing another upset, Mario relaxed. He sipped the coffee, then gestured to the owner inside the café that the coffee was acceptable. The owner beamed.

Rick poured tea the way Aunt Mandy had taught him when he was only twelve. Mario watched Rick with the degree of contempt he reserved for anyone who disagreed with him, even a beloved son-in-law.

"You like old films, Rick. Remember *Little Caesar?*"

"Starring Edward G. Robinson?"

"Don't you think it's odd that every mobster in that film was Italian?"

"Well . . ."

"Remember *Detective Story?*"

"Great flick."

"Every one of those gangsters was Italian, too."

"Every one in *The Godfather* was Italian."

"Not true. Mo Green was Jewish."

"Alright, so Mo Green was Jewish. What does that mean?"

"It means that Italians have always been considered the only gangsters in America and that's simply not fair."

Suddenly, Mario's attention was diverted as a police van arrived. The crowd called out the names of da Vinci and Columbus louder as stick-carrying policeman jumped from the van. They moved into the crowd, pushing the men, this way and that, but Italians, being very stubborn, wouldn't budge.

Quietly, Rick chanted, hoping the police wouldn't send in a SWAT team. He recognized many of the protestors. They were law-abiding natives of SoHo. Most were furious with Rick and Rosie for writing the book on the severed hands murder, but because of Mario, they would not show their anger. Rick shuddered. He'd been able to face down those Italian beasts during the hands affair because he was a black belt in karate, but he didn't want to count on continued success.

From his director's chair, Vesco pointed to the sky. The police nodded sympathetically.. Apparently, the sky was cloudy, which wasn't good for the next shot. Vesco raised his hand to his head, looking confused. The cops kept nudging the Italians. Suddenly, baseball bats appeared, smuggled from under men's jackets.

"They're going to get hurt, Mario. You've got to stop this."

"Just a few bruises, nothing much."

They watched the men bash the policeman and get bashed back. Baseball bats on the police; billy sticks on the civilians. Blood flowed and anti-Italian shouts could be heard.

"Dirty wop."

"Dago."

"Guinea."

"You see, I told you," Mario reiterated. "What language."

"Aren't you worried?"

"Naw. As long as it gets on the six o'clock news."

"So you are behind this?"

Mario's eyes bulged with innocence.

"Who, me? You know I'm a retired businessman. See, you're doing it too. My own son-in-law."

"You have a lot of influence in SoHo."

"So does the Pope," Mario retorted. Then he blessed himself for his blasphemy. "Excuse me, Father. I didn't mean it," he whispered to the sky. Then, louder, "I don't have enough influence to stop my daughter and you from writing these rotten books."

Rick decided that this was a good time for a peace talk.

"Mario, Rosie is terribly hurt. Why don't you speak to her?"

At the mention of his daughter's name, Mario began tapping on the table. Rick watched Mario's chubby fingers tapping furiously like infantry on a march.

"Why doesn't she speak to me?" Mario finally retorted between taps.

"She's called you several times."

"So, what's that. Tell her to call again. Maybe next time I'll speak to her."

"I don't understand how you can hurt her."

"She should have married an Italian. He would understand. This isn't personal, Rick. Momma always told us to marry in the blood, God rest her soul, before she died." Mario nervously blessed himself again.

"This is America. Besides Rosie loves me."

"I know, but you still don't get it."

"Get what?"

He shrugged his shoulders and motioned to the sky as if a third party were part of the conversation. Then, satisfied at a response from the heavens, Mario focused his beady eyes on Rick.

"Rick, you remember how Rosie was brought up. Our family lived in the same house. My mother and father in 3A. Aunt Lucy in 3B. Uncle Jimmy lived in 4F. Cousin Frances lived in 2A with her husband. Aunt Mary lived in 2C. Uncle

Bob in 5B. We lived in 1C. And we all had Sunday dinner together. Remember?"

Rick nodded. He'd met the family when he was sixteen. Immediately, Mario invited him to their Sunday feasts. Though they were noisy affairs, Rick had never seen a family like them. They seemed to focus their entire attention on each other and to ignore the world.

Later, they all moved to the suburbs. All except Mario.

"We were a family. We still are, but now we have to drive miles to have dinner on Sunday."

Mario wiped his forehead with an immaculate linen handkerchief. His wife, Celia, put one into his jacket pocket every morning.

"I brought Rosie up to respect her family."

"She does. We both do," Rick insisted.

"Oh, I don't expect much from you. After all, you're not Italian. But my daughter . . ." His eyes grew misty. "I never thought I'd live to see the day when she didn't respect us."

"Mario, she does respect you. All of you."

"No, she doesn't or she wouldn't write those books. Puzo started it all. Why did he have to write that book? And now he's written another one. These things are better off buried. They're in the past. Gone. It's pointless to drag them up again."

"But the hands happened only last year?" Rick began, then realized Mario was truly upset so he shut up. Instead, he grabbed the older man's hand.

"Mario, what can I do to fix things between you and Rosie?"

Mario stared sadly at Rick.

"You know, Ricky, I spent my whole life keeping these things in order. I worked hard. I was respected. I prospered. And now my daughter, my darling, is bringing up all this stuff. How am I going to face my Maker? Huh, Ricky? You tell me. How am I going to explain to God that I failed?"

7

Ice could do the mambo, the rumba, the Cuban two-step and the Spanish Harlem fly-fly, but defensively, she hugged her knees to her chest as the mock-Latino style music bellowed.

"Let Daddy show you," the tall Leather Man said as the rocking beat played on.

The two were in an apartment in Chelsea. It was a loft, furnished with several video cameras in the midst of chrome body-building equipment. On a torn-up red velvet loveseat, a frisky cat sipped cranberry juice on the rocks.

"Come on. I know you can do it for your daddy," her muscular captor said as he pet the cat.

Ice knew doing it meant strutting naked for the cameras. Uh, uh. Adamantly, she shook her curly hair. No nudies for Ice. She trashed life on her own terms, never for pigs.

"It's an art film. Come on now."

"Shit. Can it. Let me be."

Her words were not planned to evoke a lukewarm response and they didn't. The Leather Man dropped the cat to the floor and hit Ice hard at the top of her head. Tempted to slap her face, he reconsidered, not wanting to bruise her stark beauty.

It was a rare beauty, as if God had sculpted a perfect face

from white ice. Her black eyes shone like honed bits of coal, polished to shiny perfection. Her nose was small and slim. Her top lip pointed provocatively and the bottom lip was full and inviting. Her dyed blue hair was cropped in a semi-World War II crew cut except that the front bangs stood straight up at the top of her head.

It was the color of her skin that gave Ice such distinction. It was pure white and translucent and gave the illusion that its sheen could reflect like a mirror.

Around Ice was a strange white light, invisible to most, yet it conveyed to the unseeing a don't-touch ambience. For those who saw the white light, Ice inhabited a strange place of dreams, unknown realities, and exotic sensations.

The Leather Man stared at Ice, wanting her to react to his assault, but she remained calm, showing no response.

"I guess this means we gotta have another session, huh?" he crooned.

"There's nothing you can do to me that hasn't been done. Remember that, freak," Ice insisted, playing with her rags.

His eyes glittered behind the mask.

"Yeah. I got new ways to get things from ladies who are stubborn. Understand?"

"You may have new ways, but they're old ways to me," Ice said, shutting her eyes to him.

Though she was in control, she'd felt a sudden inner shudder. The man's words reminded her of her father and of the fathers in the foster families where the men always wanted to be affectionate in the wrong way. Many times her father kidnapped her and they'd run the rails until the police caught them. Her mother then would predictably go to court and commit Ice to another foster family and the same terrible scenario would begin. Her mother always wanted to get rid of Ice though she kept Tessa, Ice's undernourished younger sister. Ice often wondered why her mother hated her so.

At thirteen, Ice graduated to a teenage halfway house where she was the brassiest, most outspoken girl there. Her dark-eyed, bewildering spontaneity coupled with her vocabulary of a testy truck driver and her tendency to talk the way a cowboy shoots, impulsively and straight from the hip, made Ice few friends. Always the girl said exactly what was on her mind and some people loved that about her. They said Ice wasn't full of baloney. But Ice knew most people never said what they thought, pretending to be prim and proper above it all. Ice knew everyone was the same as everyone else, especially when they wanted sex. Sex made everybody common trash. Before she was thirteen, Ice had discovered all of this.

She began her education early. At nine, her father touched her and said it was love. That's when Ice learned that men were weak and if she was smart she could get anything she wanted. Shortly after that, Ice began an odyssey to get what she wanted from men. Strangely, only a few years later, she discovered she wanted nothing. In fact, she wanted nothing from anyone, but simply wanted to be left alone to trash her life, her way.

Now, she laughed at the Leather Man threatening her.

"Look in the mirror, Ice Goddess. You see what I got here?"

Ice didn't look up, knowing he probably had cuffs, whips, or something he thought would scare her. She knew the entire sadomasochistic repertoire cold and knew how to deal with it. Simply, she wouldn't show fear because the sadomasochistic freaks fed on that. It was their turn on.

"Yeah. Yeah. Well. Well." she said, always on center stage.

Restless, the freak tried to get his victim's attention.

"Listen, beauty. You sit around long enough and you'll get hungry and horny and do what I say."

A spiked defiance strengthened Ice's tone. She had nothing but contempt for women who posed for pornography.

"I'm not going to do what you want me to do, freak," she insisted. "I don't want to be a movie star. I don't want to make *Playboy*. They don't need me. They got all those bitches to do those things." She laughed. "I'm a goddess. Do you understand? I don't do anything I don't want to."

She emitted a gleeful yelp, clasping her hand to her mouth in feigned terror, looking both fragile and heroic as she rearranged her stark blue hair.

The Leather Man waited with whip ready, searching for a hint of fear on the young girl's lovely face. Instead, she stared him down with a look of excessive calm, bewildering every cell in his huge body. He knew Ice was trashing his threatening presence.

"I'm going to give you something special if you do what I tell you," he promised.

"I am terribly rebellious," she cooed, in an exercise of restraint.

Ice was disciplining herself, knowing she generally shot her mouth off at every inopportune moment. Instead, she was making an effort to play by the sadomasochistic rules of control and reward. That meant control of power, wholesaling fear, and then giving the victim nurturance. She'd learned about fear and reward when she'd given herself to men and made them beg for more, offering her anything for a kiss. Her sexuality was subtly constructed and minimally detailed, made to order for clients. She presented a variety of mail-order acts. By early adolescence, she was a top performer. At the height of her power, she gave it all up to learn about discipline and control. When Ice gave up sex, she made the startling realization that there was nothing anyone could get her on. She'd learned not to fear death years ago when she suffered her parents' brutality.

She laughed at the Leather Man, knowing there was nothing he could do to her.

He stood there, sensing if he used the whip she'd laugh again. Still, he attempted, whamming Ice on her buttocks. But she licked her lips and wiped him out.

Knowing she was the Grade B actress of East Second Street, Ice began to act like it. Rising from the bed, her glad rags hugged her body. They were torn where the freak had tried to undress her, and they looked like veils when she moved. She began dancing, not without a considerable number of sensuous detours. Closely, the freak watched Ice, wondering who the victim was. At every flip of her hips, he felt his energy draining.

"I'm bored to death with you, Leather Man. And I'm going now."

"No," he moaned unconvincingly.

She began to put her clothes in order, puffing up one shoulder pad, then another, using time to confuse her captor. She used this specific technique on plenty of men, the coterie of sex brokers who'd tried to pimp for her, wanting her to toil exclusively for them. They'd used drugs, force, threats, but nothing ever worked on Ice.

She trashed the Leather Man.

"I'm very la dolce vita," she hummed. "And what are you? A banana? A grape? Or are you a plum?"

The challenge fueled the man's need for escape.

"You sit around all night and trash those chums at the Snake Club, baby," he retorted. "Why don't you want to better yourself? You could make lots of bucks. I got somebody who'll make you a rich bitch."

"No. No. No." Ice replied in her singsong voice. "That's not it. You don't get it, do you, Leather Man?"

He dropped the whip and felt he wanted to worship her but didn't understand why. Disciplined in his control of women, he hadn't recognized someone with more power.

"I'm busy trashing, having kicks, freak. Life is too short for bucks."

Ice gave no second thought to his fruitless form of self-indulgence.

"Sex is for idiots," she sang. "I've got those memories, honey bun. But men have no permanent style for me."

As she moved, hitting the floor in a pulsating vivid contrast to the sea of words that she was uttering, she kicked her legs in time to the snaps of her fingers.

"Keep trashing, Leather Man," she yelled gleefully as the man moved to her count.

She was young and beautiful and she didn't care about men. She knew the more she didn't care, the more they worshipped her.

"Keep trashing, that's where it's all at," her spirit remained exuberant, her voice volcanic. "You heavy duty types don't know about real freedom. I am in control. You see what I mean."

"The Movie Man could make big bucks for you. I tell you, baby, baby," the Leather Man pleaded.

She pointed to the floor and the Leather Man got down on his knees.

"Keep on moving, Leather Man," Ice sang. "Keep on moving away from me."

Amanda looked at the collection of butter creams, marzipans, truffles, nuts, and cherries wrapped in the Limoges dish with a stark caption printed on a gold foil ribbon which read: DESSERT. The distinctive gold foil promised anyone who wanted a choco binge the utmost of pleasure. Amanda was a chocolate freak. Some of her pals were worse. She'd actually known a plastic surgeon who sent chocolate noses to potential patients to show them how the new nose would look once their own was bobbed.

Whenever Amanda set out for Felicia House, she stopped by the small elegant Madison Avenue Sweet Shoppe to pick out chocolates for the teenage girls who lived at the House. Felicia House was run by a board of directors but Amanda was the guiding force and felt responsible for it.

The tiny chocolate eggs in the top case affected Amanda. Chocolate had a mysterious hold on her. This was not true of vanilla, jelly beans, and other kinds of sweets. Generally, Amanda hated all sweets but when she looked at a dark chocolate bar, her mouth would suddenly be moist with a sudden urge to consume the bar. She had never known anything to cause this sensation, except lust. Was she a chocaholic? Probably.

She wondered what it was about the mixture of cocoa and sugar that did that. Perhaps it was because the beans were grown near a monastery on the remote slopes near Mount Kilimanjaro. Throughout the world, Amanda knew each city's best chocolate shop and often met the nicest people who were also addicts. Pitying the girls at the halfway house, Amanda always bought them a sample of elegant chocolates, hoping they would begin to see what life should be like. For Amanda believed the way to reform criminals was to drench them with luxuries. If they could switch their brilliant minds from criminality to sobriety, life would be wonderful. While the girls at the House were not real criminals, they were on their way. This current group was comprised of abandoned and molested children who chose the route of the street until Felicia House had rescued them.

"Mrs. Lord," a cheery middle-aged salesclerk smiled at Amanda. "We haven't seen you for a while."

"I've been fasting on my favorite indulgence."

"Shall I wrap one box?"

"No. Let's have a dozen. Would you mind having them brought to the car for me?"

"Right away."

Impatient, Amanda fingered the long thin chain she wore. Against her white gloves, the chain felt cold. Around her neck, Amanda wore an audacious choker of pearls from Chloe to hide the aging lines beginning to appear despite her daily massage. On her right wrist, an opulent beaded tassel bracelet designed by Valentino made a swishing sound whenever she gestured. Amanda liked whimsical combinations of accessories though her hair and dress were usually conservative. Today, she wore her hair in a neat chignon, softly puffed on each side. She covered her coquettish face with white base makeup and outlined her soft lips with apple red color. She shaded her grey eyes with mauve. Under her neat straw boater, her sultry elongated eyes gave Amanda a vibrantly exotic look. Against this exotica, her slim linen Yves

St. Laurent dress was a perfect foil. St. Laurent's new look reminded her of the fashions of the thirties, her favorite era.

"Madame. Your packages are in the car," the clerk announced.

"Thank you. You're always efficient."

As she smiled at the salesclerk, Amanda touched her diamond earrings. Good manners were like true diamonds. Long ago, her father had instructed her that good manners were simply making people comfortable. The art of good manners was her lifetime habit and while she glittered in society, Amanda's staff also always adored her. Amanda assumed that each person must feel part of the larger scheme of things, or they would be difficult to handle.

Again, she touched her diamond earrings. Rhinestones were becoming fashionable in Paris nowadays. After the Second World War, Coco Chanel had started the rage of fake pearl ropes, gold chains and Byzantine gemstones because she felt people needed to have fun. Amanda enjoyed the fakes but she agreed with the song, "Diamonds Are a Girl's Best Friend."

Yes, good manners were like diamonds. There was no substitute for class.

Back in her limo, Amanda smiled at her butler sitting on the passenger side of the front seat. Grooms was too old to drive so Amanda hired a professional chauffeur. But Grooms felt happy, sitting beside the younger man, instructing him on traffic routes. It was not an act of kindness on Amanda's part, but simply good manners.

"Grooms. Let's hurry. We're behind schedule," she said quietly.

"Please turn left," the butler instructed the driver.

Amanda was delighted at Grooms's enthusiasm. She knew what a bitter pill aging could be to a splendid body and mind. Often it had little to do with reality. Her best friend, Felicia Montremont, had died of old age at only forty. She'd been a world famous actress who had mesmerized the film world. In the fifties, she was on the cover of most major magazines. In the sixties, her legendary love affairs with most of the important wealthy and famous men of the world caused more furor. In the seventies, she died in a suspicious fire at her Adriatic hideaway in Italy.

Amanda missed Felicia's enthusiasm for life. Her regard for her fellow human beings was legendary. But Felicia could not accept growing old.

Throughout these years without Felicia, Amanda had been lonely. Generally, it was difficult for anyone to find one absolutely trustworthy friend. Amanda had found one in Felicia.

During their devoted friendship, Felicia had told Amanda of her early years as a starlet when she'd felt like an animal. Men had dehumanized her in every way possible in her climb to the top of the German film industry. Women hated her and thought her a man-stealer. Women wanted to disfigure Felicia with a knife. The clergy of her country made her a symbol of evil, so she fled to Paris where she became an international film star. When she was successful, the series of films she made when she was a teenager now began turning up to haunt her. Felicia had spent billions of dollars to take the prints off the market, but there were rumors that some still existed.

Amanda had experienced none of these humiliations. Amanda had been born in a stately white mansion in an area dotted with quaint old stone barns and stables. The Connecticut countryside was the focal point of the large house where an imposing fire was always lit in the pine-paneled living room. Off to the right was a large equipment room bursting with sporting goods, rods, creels, fishing vests and hats, tackle boxes, shooting gear, golf clubs, and tennis racquets for the robust and athletic Ramsey family. She and her brother, the Major, had lived there under the guidance of their eccentric parents who specialized in an athletic life centering on good manners, intelligent conversation, and charitable acts. When Amanda rebelled, her circle had been shocked. But she'd rebelled in a safe way among fashionable expatriates. She'd never experienced what Felicia had, never been the dangerous target of evil men's lusts. And besides, Amanda had always trained herself to be strong, both in body and in mind. She trained in karate before it was fashionable and knew most of the psychics in Europe who instructed her in the art of mind control.

Now, sitting in the rear seat of her limo, Amanda brushed tears from her eyes. Whenever she thought of Felicia, she wept. A woman had to have a best friend or life could be hell. Men could be terribly close and certainly her late husband, Eric, was, but there were certain things that only women shared. The younger generation of men were better at understanding women. Her nephew, Sonny, was gentle with his crazy Italian wife. At the thought of Rosie, Amanda began sneezing. It wasn't that she disliked Rosie, it was simply that Rosie's energy always threatened Amanda's peace of mind. Whenever Amanda met a member of the Caesare family, she felt as if she was on top of Mount Vesuvius during a lava run.

But Sonny and Rosie were happy and Amanda watched with great interest the care and concern that her nephew showered on his dramatic wife. It was almost as if he'd shed the masculine ego which marked the men of Amanda's generation. Her male friends were gentlemen, and they could be generous to women, but only if a woman held them in reverence. Even in avant-garde society, this was true.

Though Amanda knew that Sonny and Rosie were happy, many young people were not. In the last decade, there were more suicides, more drug addicts, more wandering street people among the teenage population. It was almost as if they wished to die before growing up. Amanda had created the Felicia House for these children. It was named after her dearly missed friend and she wanted it to be a place where teenage girls could learn that life can be happy.

Abruptly, the limo pulled up to the gray house on West 110th Street and Riverside Drive. Anna was standing at the door. Wearing a plaid skirt and a white blouse, Anna looked like a schoolgirl. Amanda shivered when she remembered the girl's history. At thirteen, Anna had quietly watched her boyfriend, aged fifteen, throw her mother to the floor and stab her in the neck. Since she was underage, Anna had not been tried for murder. After a series of visits to teenage facilities run by the state, Anna had come to Felicia House where Carl Collier, the director, had done wonders with her.

Anna smiled when she spotted the shopping bags filled with chocolates. She knew that the girls would prefer cigarettes and Cokes to Amanda's fancy sweets.

"Good morning, Mrs. Lord." Anna called out.

"How are you?"

Slowly, they walked into the hallway of the house.

"I'm going to take the word-processing course," Anna replied, knowing that the acquisition of work skills made Amanda happy.

"Wonderful."

The entrance hallway had thick marble pillars that reached to the high ceilings. The house had been a bordello in the twenties and Amanda had bought it when the area began going downhill. It was perfect for the halfway house because it had five floors and many bedrooms. Amanda hoped the girls would never find out what the house had originally been used for.

She'd often thought of how different the Felicia girls were from those brought up twenty blocks away on Park Avenue. There, girls were spoiled princesses. Their parents were affluent and obsessed by their own climb to the top. With fierce determination these families felt nothing was too good for their children. From prekindergarten age, the girls were primed to take their place in society. Although these days girls were encouraged to have a profession, marriage to the right kind of boy was their first goal.

But the Felicia girls were from society's slums. Many were illegitimate. Many, like Anna, had been witnesses to horrendous crimes. To most, family violence and abuse was common. One of the girls had been put on the street to sell her body at the age of eight. Amanda shuddered at these humiliations.

Amanda was determined the Felicia girls would turn out differently. They were clothed, given schooling, good food and therapy by Carl Collier.

"Mrs. Lord," Carl Collier called from his office. "I didn't expect you today."

"I thought I'd pop by with some chocolates."

As he joined Amanda, Carl smiled. The girls often talked about her chocolates in therapy and saw the sweets as the decadence of the rich.

"How is everything?" Amanda asked.

Carl took one of Amanda's gloved hands and kissed it, knowing it was a gesture she loved.

"Wonderful. The words processing class has turned out to be the most popular. Some of the girls are already earning money. Collier Films has given us PR material."

"Your brother's firm?"

He laughed. "Film companies are always behind in their mail so the girls are earning pin money."

He pointed to a room on the left. Amanda looked through the glass window to see several girls operating a word processor.

"Fine," she said.

"Can you stay for tea?"

"I'm sorry. I'm late for another appointment. But I'll see you at the board meeting next week."

They began walking to the door.

"How have you been?"

"Awful. The police are causing me difficulty."

"Yes. I read about that in the newspapers. It must have been an awful experience."

"Thank heavens, my nephew was with me."

"Rick Ramsey is your nephew?"

"Yes. I'm proud of him. He wrote that best-selling book on those awful Italian severed hands."

"Yes, I read the book, but I didn't know he was your nephew."

"Well, I've got to dash."

After Amanda left, Collier, troubled, walked back into his office. The media had not identified Ramsey as Amanda Lord's nephew. Rick Ramsey might cause trouble if he poked around Amanda's affairs. Collier picked up the phone and dialed.

9

"Damn. Damn. Damn." Rosie swore.

She was dressed in her interviewing outfit: taupe slouch hat, taupe knit top, taupe pegged pants, taupe low heels. Rosie claimed that the blandness of taupe encouraged people to blab.

"Damn!" she swore again.

Annoyed, she threw her large taupe bag to the floor, which caused a loud crackling sound.

"You've destroyed the tape recorder," Rick observed.

"Damn those cops."

"Nice people."

"Don't kid around," she said, tearing her clothes off.

The loft was hot. On schedule, the air conditioning unit had broken down as it did every year during humid weather. Rosie said it was because the SoHo building wanted to restate its origin and remind tenants that they were simply humans, and struggling humans, at that.

Carefully, she put her clothes into a neat pile, tipping Rick off that she was upset. Rosie liked order. Upon disrobing, she always hung up her clothes.

Rick waited for the holocaust of Italian fury which was about to erupt. While waiting, he jogged to the fridge for a Coke.

"God damn it," Rosie swore again.

Smiling, Rick handed Rosie her favorite addiction: Coke.

"You'll feel better if you get mad. Get mad."

"It's Kushel. You think after we solved the severed hands crime, he'd be nicer."

"What is he doing now?"

"He's blaming us for making his life miserable. He says if it wasn't for your jogging discovery, he might never have to speak to the Mafia. Can you imagine his gall? He told me he graduated from Notre Dame and went to NYU Law School before he dropped out so that he would never have to deal with Italians. Kushel, it seems, thinks being Lithuanian is the gift of the gods, or he thought so, until he met my father."

"I'm getting to like Kushel."

"You're *très* sentimental."

"He was helpful last time. We made our peace with him when we brought in the murderer. I miss Kushel."

"Miss him? Rick, when are you going to stop sounding like a morning soap opera?"

"Rosie," Rick said patiently, "get out your anger. Go ahead, scream."

She screamed.

"Do it again."

She screamed again.

Suddenly, there was a loud chugging sound from the top floor of the building. Rick knew it was Arnoldo's robot. The robot had been created by the sculptor last year and had been instrumental in saving Rosie's life in their last caper. Ever since that time, the robot watched protectively over Rosie so much so that Arnoldo had changed it from female to male.

"He must have heard your scream," Rick said.

He picked up the phone and dialed Arnoldo's number.

"Tell the electronic chap that she's all right," Rick said into the phone. "She's simply screaming."

When he placed the phone back on the receiver, Rick smiled.

"Arnoldo says his robot is in love with you."

"How sweet."

"Do you want to scream again?"

Rick was happy that he'd read all the books on self-help: how to be happy, how to be angry, how to be sexual, how to be rich, how to be anything you want to be, because it gave him behavior tactics which seemed to work on that strangest of all people, the Italians.

Now, Rosie smiled at him.

"Did you find out anything, luv?" he asked, knowing Rosie had been to the police.

"Uh, huh."

"What?"

"That breastless body was Baby Sue Ellen Compton. She was from St. Louis, Missouri, and wanted to be a country-western singer. Well, she saved up her baby-sitting money and took a slow bus to Manhattan and got here in time to meet a pimp named Hoofer Harris, named because he used to be a starving dancer before he became a rich pimp. Hoofer Harris met Baby Sue and promised he'd get her a job singing in a famous café if she was nice to him. Baby Sue believed him and went the route with Hoofer."

"The route?"

"Hmmm. You know the scenario. Kushel tells it this way: Hoofer bought Baby Sue to dinner, bought her fancy duds, and introduced her to the top lady of his hooker business, who happened to live with Hoofer and the other little hookers. Then, Hoofer told the girls that he was in love with Baby Sue and took her into his bedroom and got Baby Sue hooked on him. Are you following me?"

"Perfectly. In Connecticut, we read dirty novels early."

Rosie laughed.

"Well, anyhow the top lady broke Baby Sue into the art of doing tricks on the streets of our lovely city. The poor kid became the local specialist in whippings and sadomasochistic stuff." Rosie looked suddenly pained.

"How could that happen? Rick? How could a kid named

Baby Sue become a specialist at sadomasochistic stuff at seventeen?"

"Maybe it happened to her at home?"

"God. My father wouldn't let anyone look at me, let alone touch me. That poor girl."

"How did they identify her?"

"From her teeth. It seems she had something wrong with her jaw and was x-rayed back in St. Louis."

"Did she ever sing?"

"Yes. Hoofer got her a gig at the Snake Club."

"That cave."

"We've got to go there and check this out."

"Right."

"But there's a new twist to the scenario."

"What's that?"

"Hoofer Harris's decomposed body was found thirty miles from the city. He'd been shot in the head while wearing a blue satin frock coat like the kind Elton used to wear before he got married."

"So, no leads?"

"We'll have to talk to the other girls in Hoofer's harem."

"Rosie, they're notoriously closemouthed."

The phone rang. On the other end, Aunt Mandy spoke earnestly.

"Sonny, there's police everywhere. I thought we had a new doorman but it seems that Ramon has been relieved after all this time, because a policeman is watching over my home. Imagine, Sonny? We're in a difficult time when the police authorities can insist that they be on private property twenty-four hours a day."

"I, for one, am glad. Then, I know you're protected."

"From what, luv? I can fend for myself, you know. Last time we had a robbery, they tied up Grooms but, when they got to me, I hit them on the head with that baseball bat that Rosie's father—achooo—Mr. Caesare—achooo—gave me to protect myself when he heard I was living alone in a Park Avenue—achooo—penthouse."

"Stop sneezing. Haven't you gotten used to my in-laws yet?"

"Achooo! Achooo!"

"Mandy. Calm yourself."

"I wish Eric were here now. He'd know what to do."

"I know you miss him."

Rosie was listening to Rick's end of the conversation with a look of disdain on her face. She'd already identified the fact that another Ramsey was speaking to Rick, because her husband spoke in a manner which was absolutely foreign to SoHo and came from somewhere in the bowels of Connecticut, a place Rosie hated and vowed never to visit.

"You're sweet, Sonny. Rosie—achooo—is very lucky. You tell that Italian girl, that she is—achooo—very lucky."

"You're very lucky, Rosie," Rick told his wife.

"I think you're the lucky one, darling," she said, sticking out her tongue adorably.

"Do you want to speak to Rosie, Aunt?"

"Achooo. Achooo."

"Tell her to use a handkerchief," Rosie quipped, knowing of Mandy's strange allergic reaction to anything Italian.

"I'll come and see you tomorrow. I'll talk to the police and ask them to stop harassing you. Alright, Aunt Mandy?"

"Achooo. Yes, Sonny, darling. I love you."

"I'm mad for you, sweetie."

After he hung up, Rosie asked, "Rick, is leather in style again?"

"I don't know anyone who still wears leather."

"Funny, that's what I thought. But lately, it's leather, leather, leather."

She shrugged her shoulders.

"Must be the guys on the set. California is always behind SoHo."

"Some of them do wear leather," she agreed. "Hey, did I tell you that Miles says I don't have to do any more rewrites?"

"Great."

"Miles loves everything I wrote and told Bains that he wants the money. When Bains stalled, Miles said, listen you jock bastard, you pay Rosie Caesare or you won't get another comma out of her. Miles said he can control Bains."

"Miles can control anyone."

"And Miles said that our editor at Bulloughs, Melissa Adams, wants the new book."

"Do we have a new book?"

"Of course. I call it *The Severed Breasts*."

"It has a nice ring to it."

"Let's go out and dine and celebrate."

"I'd rather be alone with you."

"Oh, well, there's the zucchini."

"Let's make one of your outrageous pastas."

"Into the kitchen with you."

They held hands as they walked to the kitchen area which was now furnished with the style of a Caribbean villa. Everything was hot pink, even the stove and fridge, which Rosie had had painted over. This area had formerly been decorated as part of the Sistine Chapel, but when Rosie and Rick finished *The Severed Hands* book which was now the film, *SoHo Vice*, she said she'd had it with things Italian and was looking for peace and quiet, lush sounds, gorgeous hot colors and mostly not being cold. That's when she thought of the Caribbean motif.

"I want us to be fulfilled," she announced as she chopped the zucchini with a large knife.

"But we are, aren't we?"

"It's important for us to have a positive image and be morally good people. I think we have Kushel's respect because we're married and we're equal, don't you think?"

"I think he likes us because we're rich and famous."

"You may be famous, but you're a peach."

"You're real sexy, do you play the drums?"

She laughed.

"Rick, I think Baby Sue was the kind of girl who handpicked the man to deflower her."

"How do you know that?"

"From Kushel. Kushel says New York City is not a sexy city because people buy sex here. He says even when they call it relating there's a price tag on it."

"Don't believe everything you hear from the Lithuanian."

"You're beginning to sound like Dad."

"I consider that a compliment."

"Dad wanted to save me from the grim facts of life and Kushel says that finding hands and stuff are leading us down to the slimy side of life. Kushel says that whenever he sees Dad, Kushel is told he has to protect us."

"The water's boiling."

Rosie picked up the fresh pasta from Raffettos on West Houston Street. She'd bought the whole wheat kind because she was a health nut and though she loved all delicacies from Italy, she substituted the new healthy versions. She waited quietly at the stove with a look that Rick had seen on the face of her mother, Celia, whenever Celia was boiling pasta. It was a semi-worried look, as if the pasta would not do well unless the cook cared. Rick looked into the pot. The water began swirling. On cue, Rosie tossed the dark fettucini into it. Without missing a beat, she stir-fried the zucchini in a wok. Then she turned to the large pot, carried it to the sink, poured the mixture out into the strainer and quickly tossed the pasta into the zucchini in the wok. She stirred up the whole mess quickly, and carried the wok to the table where Rick had laid out plates and utensils.

When Rick tasted it, he raved.

"This is delicious. How do you do it?"

"It's easy. Try it some time."

"I've tried. I can't do it. You do it easily."

"I was trained early," she said with bitterness.

As they dined, Rosie began to list things that she simply didn't think worked in films any longer.

"I don't like dressing weird and acting strange," she began.

"What about *Body Heat?*"

"Kathleen Turner wore much too much mascara. Mascara is definitely out these days."

"What else is out, darling?"

"Suntans. Very long nails. Being too thin."

He squeezed her and she slapped his hand playfully as she continued.

"Perms. Cropped hair for men. And Gene Hackman."

"Gene is out?"

"Yup. Also, playing the piano perfectly. Some people think you have to play the piano perfectly in order to make an impression on your audience. But that's not so. Concerts have been memorable when all notes were not perfect."

"George Winston's notes are all perfect."

"Mostly."

To illustrate her esoteric point, Rosie danced over to the piano where she proceeded to play Lorenz Hart's "The Lady Is a Tramp," hitting a few clinkers in the process. Rick felt good, knowing Rosie must be happy. Rosie could only play the piano when she was feeling good. He walked over to her and kissed the back of her neck, causing her to shiver deliciously.

"Would you love me if we were beyond sex?" she asked.

"How do you mean?"

"Like Jake Barnes in *The Sun Also Rises*, that book which was a movie and is now a TV movie."

"What about Jake?"

"Well, he was impotent but Brett still loved him."

"But she screwed everybody around."

"What does that matter? Jake lost his equipment so he couldn't make love. But he loved her. I think that's the sweetest and dearest thing a man can do for a woman."

"What's that?"

"Accept her totally."

"Come again."

"Rick," she said impatiently, "if a man can't have sex with a woman and he still loves her, then he really loves her. Don't you see that?"

10

Producer Ed Bains sat at a lawn table at his Long Beach waterfront estate, reading the script rewrites for *SoHo Vice*, a Collier Film production, his entry into the world of Class A films.

"Jesus," he said to the film's director, Vesco, "What is this crap? I thought the Mafia hoods were going to take the heat?"

"Haven't you read the book?"

"Don't have any goddamn time to read," Bains slammed the script hard down on the table, causing a grapefruit cup to splatter his white linen shirt. Before he could complain, two manservants wiped up the mess. He grunted and waved them away.

"Vesco, I repeat, I thought this was going to be a hood picture."

"It is."

"You know how much money *The Godfather* made. I want that kind of gold."

"Well," Vesco said, "I need the $800,000 for the extra crew. That's why I'm here. They've got to get paid today."

"How can you ask me for more money?" Bains screamed. "Leave me alone. Don't do this to me."

"Remember? I discussed this with you. I explained we'd

save money in the long run if we have the second-unit crew take the Manhattan shots. That way I can concentrate on SoHo where all the dramatic action takes place. You agreed."

Bains shook his head, then fingered the blue sapphire pinky ring he wore because it matched the pool water.

"I can't do it. You've got enough money from me. Go someplace else."

Vesco shook his head. It was eleven A.M., not a good time for the producer, who generally did not sleep but spent the night satisfying the various appetites of the human body, which Vesco did not want to contemplate. A graduate of a prestigious film school, Vesco had been chosen to direct *SoHo Vice* because his last film, *The Torturer*, had grossed top money all over the country. Hollywood was buzzing that Vesco really knew how to make gun films.

"Look, I'm doing you a favor. I don't want to call out the unions because then we'll have a shutdown and the picture will never be finished on time. You agreed to produce this picture. I don't care where you get the money as long as the budget is met. You wanted to keep all the numbers. Okay. Then cough up the money. If you don't want to do that, we can go to a studio and get a distribution deal. But this really isn't my job. I don't have the percentage points. I'm simply an employee, working on salary."

Though the younger man gestured wildly, he was trying not to patronize the Wall Street genius. Vesco was always surprised when billionaires acted like dime-store operators, which they often did with movie people. Vesco vowed to get out of the business of begging for money, the way others like Coppola had, by breaking out of the studio system. He had a plan to do his own films, but at this time, the plan was still secret. He dreamed of the time when he could become a filmmaker in the world he really cared about: the gay world.

There was a good profit in being gay these days, and about time. Gays gave other gays business. It was happening all over the country. A new gay bank in San Francisco. Gay computer services. Gay printing presses. Real estate. All gays coming out of the closet to tap the gay market. It was a marketing dream and Vesco wanted in.

His problem was how to establish a gay Class A film industry. Except for films of great literary works, the gay lifestyle was not first-run film material. There were a few exceptions like the brilliant *Sunday Bloody Sunday*, but they were not the norm for Hollywood.

It would be difficult to establish a major film on this sexual preference but Vesco was determined to do it, although his reputation as a successful director of macho films preceded him. He had to change his image, to make himself bankable as a sensitive director of this alternative life-style. He had a long-range plan to do this, and *SoHo Vice*'s success was an important part of it.

Vesco turned to his jock producer. Out at the wharf landing, Bains's private yacht, named "The Happy Stud," was tied up. The boat was equipped with women and other essentials of pleasure. Vesco had had to perform before getting his contract. He'd performed very well because he liked women.

Vesco watched Bains struggling with his anger.

"This script is crap. Who's going to believe those killings? Cutting off hands. Naw." He gestured savagely at crotch level.

"Ed, we've got to follow the book's plot line."

"Why? For Christ's sake, this is a movie."

"Jesus, Ed. We can't change the ending. Besides, Rick Ramsey just found another body. This one has no breasts. They'll probably write another book. If it makes the bestseller list we could do another deal with them. We don't want the writers to get mad at us, do we?"

"Yeah, I heard about the new body," Bains paused. "I tell you this, Stu baby. I'm not happy. And when I'm not happy . . ."

Vesco knew that his expensive crew was waiting for him, lighting part of West Broadway for the next shot.

"Ed, I've got to get back to the city. If I don't, it'll cost us a fortune."

"You're making me crazy."

Bains rose from the breakfast table and began stalking the terrace, walking, then jogging, up and down, back and forth. Vesco watched his producer pitch up his fury. This guy is a weirdo, Vesco thought. He liked to have utter confusion around him all the time. Vesco knew that Bains had gone over the script thoroughly and approved everything in it. Rosie Caesare had done rewrites. It was a good script. And his direction would make the movie terrific. He'd make money and a name for himself if *SoHo Vice* was ever released. Everyone attached to the picture had a special fondness for the project because it was fun, weird, bloody, and sexy. What else did a blockbuster need?

"Ed, I'm waiting for your answer."

"Okay, okay, don't bother me anymore."

Bains waved the director away but Vesco stood firm.

"We're paying that actor too much money," Bains continued complaining. "Fifty thousand a week with a guarantee of five weeks. Who is he?"

"He's hot. We've nailed him before his price goes sky-high. Believe me, we got a bargain there. We only have another week to go. Don't stop now, for God's sake."

Vesco knew that everyone connected with the film was flying first-class, renting limousines, and that wardrobe, makeup, hairstyle, and catering costs had skyrocketed. But he also knew that everyone was too far into the picture to back out now.

"Ed, will the money be there for the crew?"

"Yeah, yeah, don't bother me. Go ahead. Get out of here. But I'm watching you all the way to the bank, fella. Remember that," the producer threatened.

"I'm not in charge of the damn budget. I shouldn't even be here talking about the money. I'm the director."

"What you are, baby face, is my gofer. You come when I tell you, you go when I tell you, do you get my drift?"

Vesco held down the rage that was building inside of

him, praying that after he got the Oscar he could avoid men like Bains.

"Are you finished making me feel bad, Ed?" he said quietly.

"That Caesare cunt. She stood me up the other day. Who the hell does she think she is?"

"I don't know, Ed. Her agent is screaming about the fact that we didn't pay her for the rewrites yet. Do you want to get into it with him now? Or do we tidy up the film first, then go to court?" Vesco answered snidely.

"Look, I haven't started making trouble. Go ahead. Go back to your picture." Bains picked up the script and threw it at Vesco. "Only I want the hoods to be the murderers. Understand?"

"There's no way we can do that."

"You do it, Stu, baby. You do it for me."

As Bains watched the handsome young director leave, he laughed. He'd been easy on Vesco because of his avowed new style, to be smooth instead of bullheaded. A former tournament drinker, host of extravagant international parties and a five-time husband, Bains was assuming a life of casual restraint now, because he'd given up the bottle and was collecting the rubble of his personal life. But he still loved young ass. That, he would never give up.

His roughness was acceptable because of his legacy of Wall Street money and because he traveled the posh playgrounds of the world. Now, as always, there was a play of contrasts on his face, his ruddy complexion evoking his former dissipated life-style. In other centuries, his kind of man probably didn't last long. They wore themselves out with too much sex and alcohol. He couldn't give up sex so he'd given up the sauce in his bid for immortality.

Bains had spent most of his life studying world economics and female adaptability, his two obsessions. He envied women because the female trait of adaptability made them endure. He invented special scenarios for the female sex, learning how to exercise power and be a masculine take-charge man. In other words, an s.o.b.

Most women loved it. Every year of his life had gotten better because he understood more about himself. When he was younger he was bluntly outspoken. To press his case, he needed to feel challenged. He'd defeated Wall Street, now he would defeat Hollywood.

He planned to live a long life because of dieting, lifting weights, skipping rope, and other exercises requiring discipline. It was the same discipline that required him to buy and sell in various degrees of speculation on the world markets. Money kept his animal energy percolating.

And there was the shadowy world that was his secret pleasure: the fascinating world of pornography. This world taught him excitement with restraint. Because he was a busy man, he didn't have time to kid around with dating and marriage and that kind of thing. It took too long to educate various women into his likes and dislikes, his screams of obscenity, his brutal longings. His wives had divorced him for his proclivities, but he didn't care. Not one had gotten a dime from him.

He took a certain bittersweet pleasure in his success in the porno business run by a subsidiary of Collier Films, but had a jaundiced view of the Class A film business. Most stars were pains in the asses who were destructive to everyone around them. Directors were worse. There was a childishness to all film people. Even though they used a free exchange of affection, most of them hated each other. Locations used up all of their lives, six days a week, twelve hours a day, keeping their ego energy percolating. Between films, most of them were anxious and bored so producers could manipulate them.

Bains was the best manipulator in the world. He saw himself as a slim-hipped modern-day gladiator, a man with dash. Every day was a fight into his universe.

Then there was his other life.

He liked to beat up women and liked to watch other men do it, too. Sometimes, he even liked to watch women beat up women, though that was harder to find. But it wasn't until he visited his friend, the Colonel, in Buenos Aires, that he was introduced to the delicate eroticism of teenagers. When a woman looked into his eyes after he'd given her a whipping, she looked defeated. When a girl looked at him after he'd trained her in the art of complete obedience, she wore a look of admiration. This was a great difference.

A woman would scheme revenge afterwards and he had to keep up his guard. Or a woman would become completely passive and boring. On the other hand, a girl played it all like a game and delighted in new ways of pleasing her "papa." He loved it when they called him that. The Brazilian girls said it with much flavor. When the Colonel invited him to indulge in orgies, Bains had returned home realizing that not only were there millions of pleasures in the girl business, but there were also billions of dollars.

The modeling agencies had started it. Everywhere there were kids for sale. Child models. Child actors. These kids were devils with a certain mischief. Always, they needed attention. They were tough but they folded easily. They took orders well. Bains took it one step further. He began financing pornographic films, specializing in teenagers. Then Collier, his partner, had had a brainstorm and they began publishing books and magazines, and opening clubs. Bains had been amazed at the huge audience of pedophiles. He became a connoisseur, sending his agents around the world to find very special talent under eighteen.

That's how he'd heard about Ice.

Leather Man had been watching Ice for sometime. He'd reported that.

She had talent. Bains had gone to the Snake Club in disguise and watched Ice's trashing act. He agreed that she was something special and gave the Leather Man an order for her.

But he wanted her undamaged. Sometimes Leather Man got too involved in what he was doing and spoiled the merchandise.

11

The barren beach was gray on this unusual summer day. Torn beach umbrellas from the sudden rainstorm littered the sand. The sky was still dark when Ice's taxi pulled up to the small cottage that was too warm in summer, too cold in winter, and a bad place to live.

Inside the cottage, Ice was in a rage.

"I told you if you let anyone touch my baby sister I'd kill him."

Violently she shook her mother.

"How can you? What kind of a mother are you?"

Linda Martin shrieked. Her dark eyes were bleak and her gaunt face revealed that life was hell.

"Tessa is lying."

"Linda, get sensible. Look at her."

Tessa was lying on a threadbare couch, crying. Ice was mad at her, and she didn't quite understand what she had done wrong. She'd tried to be a good girl and obeyed her stepfather. Isn't that what her mother had wanted her to do? Linda always said, Ralph is your father now, Tessa. You must obey him the way you obey me. So, when her mother was out working at the local Grand Union, and her stepfather asked her to do those things, she never thought she should say no. She wanted to tell Ice about those things before, but everytime Ice visited, there was violent quarreling so Tessa never got a chance to speak.

Today was accidental. Unexpectedly, Ice had stopped by. Ralph hadn't expected anyone so they were secluded in the bedroom, and Ralph was stroking Tessa with what she called his peanut.

"I love you," he murmured as he explored her. "This is good touching, isn't it?" he asked the naive fifteen-year-old girl.

"It doesn't hurt anymore, Ralph. Just like you said."

"Does it feel good?"

"Yes."

She knew that Ralph felt happy when she said that his peanut felt good inside her. But it didn't make her feel that way. When he'd first showed her this game she was seven and it really hurt. But Ralph had been very patient and stopped whenever she asked him to. Now, Tessa was used to it. But today, Ralph had wanted to do something new and scared Tessa. So she'd screamed.

At that moment, Ice entered the beachfront cottage. Startled, Ralph jumped up, put on jeans and a sweater, and told Tessa to keep quiet. But Ice came to the doorway and hell had broken loose so Ralph climbed out of the window and ran down the beach.

Ice screamed at him through the window.

"You bastard."

Then she hurried to her sister.

"Are you alright?"

"Yes. Why are you mad?"

"Baby, does he do that a lot?"

"Whenever Momma works overtime."

"When will she be home?"

"In a half hour."

Ice and Tessa spent the next hour talking. When Linda strolled in, carrying two huge bags of groceries, Ice grabbed her mother roughly and the groceries fell all over the kitchen.

Ice was in a rage, tears falling uncontrollably down her cheeks.

"Are you an animal? You let my father ruin my life. Now Ralph is ruining Tessa. Tessa, get your things. You're coming to the city with me."

Linda flinched. Turning from Ice, she took a cigarette from the pack on the kitchen counter, lit it, and blew smoke into Ice's face.

"Tessa probably asked for it, like you did. You were always flirting with your father. For God's sake, you're the reason we broke up. After you were born, he was never the same. He couldn't take his eyes off you. When I told him I was having Tessa, he left me. But he kept on coming back to see you, you bitch."

Ice calmly picked up a steak knife from the kitchen counter.

"No, don't, Bonni," Tessa screamed.

Ice melted.

"Go get your things."

"Where you going to take her to? That basement? Where you live with the rats?"

"Rats are better than the scum you live with."

"Don't say that about Ralph."

Ice looked at the kitchen floor littered with cookies, taffy, popcorn, ice cream, TV dinners, bought by a mother who didn't care a damn for her kids.

"Are you sure you're our mother?" Ice asked.

"I didn't know it was happening," Linda screamed.

"That's not good enough." Ice bit her lip. She was restraining herself from stomping Linda like cyclists always did in gang wars.

"If you ever see my father, tell him I'll kill him," she threatened.

"Don't lie to me. You love him."

"I don't."

But Ice was lying, for somehow she did love him.

"You would run off with him all the time," Linda complained bitterly.

"It was better than being here with all those strange goons coming in and out of the bedroom. When Ralph moved in I told you to lay down the law or I'd take Tessa away."

"I'll call the cops."

"You do it and I'll tell them how you stood by and watched your daughters being raped. They'll put you away, mother dear."

"I had to take it. My uncles. All of them when I was a kid." Linda began weeping. "Ralph promised me he'd never touch Tessa. Baby, did he hurt you?"

"Get away from her," Ice screamed.

"You filth," Linda swung at Ice.

But Ice was too fast for her and blocked her blows.

"I'm filth? I may trash my life. I may live in a basement, but I don't let any goon touch me, and I won't let any goon touch my baby sister."

Ice looked at her anorectic sister whose large eyes dominated her face, as Linda's did. Tessa's limbs were reed thin though she sported the appetite of a truck driver.

"Come on, sweet sis," Ice put her arm around the frail girl.

"Where are you taking her?"

"None of your business and if you try to interfere, Ice will make trouble for you," Ice threatened.

In the cab, Tessa shook the sense of dread away, the way children often did, for though she was fifteen, Tessa was very childlike.

"Bonni, can we have McDonald's? And a fudge sundae?"

"Don't call me Bonni, honey. I'm known as Ice in the city."

"Where to?" the driver asked.

"East Second Street. Right off First Avenue."

The driver looked into the mirror to stare at Ice again. Her black leather short skirt was fringed with sequins. The soft black mesh top she wore was torn at the armpits. Her black lace stockings, strewn with sequins, were also torn. She wore short black elf boots which gave a childlike appearance to her starkly sexual costume. In her hair, she had bows and knots of every color, pulling at her one way and then another. Around her neck she wore glass baubles sprinkled with jet beads and gold stones.

The driver swore, his excitement mounting as he drove to the city.

"When we get home, we'll go out and get you a special bed, okay?" Ice said.

"Is anyone there?" Tessa asked.

"Where?"

"At your house?"

"Just us," Ice said sweetly. "We're going to live there and be happy."

"How about Mom?"

"She'll be okay. She's got that goon, Ralph."

"But I always cook for her."

"She'll have to learn how to boil potatoes. You're going to go to school. You know you love to dance. The city has great schools for that kind of thing."

"Can we afford it?"

"Don't worry about the cash. Your Ice will take care of that."

"I love you, Bonni."

Ice grimaced at her birth name. After she'd lost her virginity, she'd changed her name to Ice. It seemed appropriate. Her given name had been Bonni and after she'd gotten into the weird excitement of New Wave and Hard Core she made a decision to do complete surgery on her personality. Not only did she trash her life, her clothes, her makeup, her jewelry, but also her name.

She remembered the day the proper name had come to her. Ice. It was how she felt most of the time.

Ice had come to life on the threshold of innocence like the rest of the human race, but somehow her experience preceded her biological growth because she was drawn into a world of sexuality and debasement before most kids graduate from grammar school. Because of her youth, it was a while before she realized that this life was not the only reality. As she passed through the common practice of adults inflicting pain upon their children, it seemed to Ice that this was the way of the world.

So she made some important decisions.

She refused to be drawn into the world of sexual expertise offered to her. She reversed her history. If she had been older, she would have ended up in a bordello. But she was of a younger generation, born into the urgent video pop world where Michael Jackson and Prince were the kings who triumphed over life by becoming mysterious erotic holy men, who trashed all kinds of emotions and still survived. These glittering superstars were Ice's background motif as each night, with the fervor of an evangelist, she trashed all sides of her spiritual and emotional nature. Nothing was sacred. Only a belief in magic remained Ice's prayer. If her life was trashed, then the fact that she survived was magical. This was acceptable to her.

Ice blamed all pain on adults. The grownups had caused this pain and the radical fringe reacted violently. Adults and children were at war. Books about the killing of children made the best-seller lists. And in the real world, children were killing their parents. Where the seventies had recorded the battle of the sexes, the eighties recorded the battle between parents and children. And the issue of child abuse and molestation, once hidden in the closet, was becoming the main issue of this nightmare time.

Ice knew all of this. She read every magazine and newspaper and watched the TV news. It gave her a background reality to trash her life with. Ice also read books. Her closets in the Second Street basement were lined with intellectual works. Ice understood them, for she had a natural intellect, a poetic sensibility. But she preferred the seamy side of life where things seemed purer than the elaborateness of Fifth Avenue's Trump Tower.

When Ice wasn't trashing, she spent most of her time in bookstores, going through lists of books she had not read, hoping to find someone to tell her of another way of life, one that she could hold on to and not feel decadent.

Books, music, and magic pulled Ice through her awesome reality. An adult at seventeen, she wasn't afraid of anything. She'd done drugs, sex, and violence and now was embarked on a magical journey to come up on the other side of reality, as *Dante's Inferno* had promised. She hoped it would be soon.

As the taxi crossed the bridge, the Manhattan skyline came into view, an awesome challenge. To Ice, the sight gave comfort. Only in Manhattan, in the dark recesses of the Lower East Side, was she permitted to be herself.

"Can I wear that skirt?" Tessa tugged at Ice's short leather mess.

"When you're older."

As Ice looked into her sister's eyes, they so resembled her mother's that she felt a flush of hatred for the woman who had borne them both. While Tessa looked like Linda, Ice looked like her father, John. She thought she and Tessa must make a strange portrait. Two bedraggled children, arms about each other, going out in a world of sin, corruption, and slaughter, yet aiming to survive.

Suddenly, Ice pulled her sister to her and kissed her on the forehead. She was overcome with a warm sickly feeling that she couldn't identify. And with that feeling came panic. She'd never had to care for another human being. She trashed everyone in her life, including her friends. Now she would have to care for Tessa.

Would she be able to do it?

12

To make her first appearance at the Snake Club where trashy rags were a staple, Rosie chose a "Dynasty" dress of red crepe satin, a wraparound flirt dress with rhinestone beading along the neckline and topped off by an Alexis Carrington chunky necklace. On her wedding ring finger, she wore an Alexis ring, rhinestones and black onyx.

"I'm going as a bitch," she said.

"You look like a bitch."

"Are you wearing that thing?"

"It's a perfectly good match to your outfit."

"But you can wear that at the Harvard Club. Do something different to it."

Rick examined his evening tux. Aside from wearing Nikes, he couldn't think of anything else.

"Wear the rhinestone tie."

"Rosie, I'm not into that."

"For tonight."

She handed him a red rhinestone tie that matched her "Dynasty" dress.

"I bought this for you this afternoon," she said, flirtatiously.

"Then I shall have to wear it."

She laughed as she dressed her hair into a severe roll, like Krystal Carrington, but spun the bangs into tiny ringlets like Alexis's.

"I see you can't decide between Linda and Joan," Rick joked.

"They're both glorious."

"According to the most recent studies an outrageously bold woman is a bitch. That's you, my darling."

"I don't like the term."

"A woman like you is an out-front woman. A woman who is not afraid to go after what she wants."

"The way I went after you."

"I thought I pursued you."

"Ha ha."

"Do I have to wear this tie?"

"It looks delicious. Now, remember Ricky, tonight we are going into a den of iniquity."

"*Casbah*. Tony Martin. Peter Lorre. Nineteen forty-eight."

"Right. Like the Casbah, the Snake Club will reveal the secret rituals of the lower-class jet set."

"What's that?"

"The underbelly of the city. The dark regions of its surrealistic unconscious. The waves of energy that grow in the belly of the Lower East Side and spring forth, sprouting the universal truths which will grow into the "Dynasties" of tomorrow.

"Huh?"

Rick was puzzled. Every once in a while Rosie had esoteric bouts of reality and used poetical philosophical descriptions which completely puzzled him. He decided this was due to her early reading of Dante. After all, reading that guide to Italian nirvana, *The Inferno*, when she was only ten must have done something to her inner psyche. According to Dante, there was much pain and suffering laid out for the living. Rick had tried to read this masterpiece but it constantly offended his puritan conscience. He was more comfortable with Camus, who also instructed everyone to be blue but at least began to toy with the idea that pain was of one's own making. Dante, on the other hand, gave Rick the impression that there was no avoidance of pain and suffering if one chose to live.

This was Mario's philosophy, too. Of course, he had diligently instructed Rosie in it. But Rosie, being modern and living very much in the present, had already figured out that pain was worth avoiding, if possible. Rosie, however, made the distinction that it was never possible to sidestep conflict, which was life. But she felt that a compassionate nature coupled with courage could bring a person through anything. Rick, on the other hand, did good things because of duty and felt Rosie was the more humane of the two.

He examined his wife. Rosie was immersed in a red sequined cape she'd borrowed from the transvestite who owned the grocery store on the corner. Emile wore lots of shiny red while he sold fresh vegetables and fruits to SoHoites.

"I've been reading lots of research on skeletons."

"Oh, changing the subject?"

"Not really. It seems there was a truck driver who was supposed to be incinerated in a gas tank explosion. His wife had a double indemnity insurance policy so naturally the police were suspicious. Well, they had a skeleton expert look at the bones and he discovered they were the bones of a pig. So, the victim was obviously hiding out somewhere waiting for his wife to collect the cash. Isn't that interesting?"

"Isn't what interesting?"

"That they can identify almost anyone from the skeleton. Like you. You're a runner so the patterns on your pelvis would reveal that you are an athlete. And do you know something else?"

"What?"

"Knobby bumps on the jawbone can reveal that the person played a wind instrument. Stress marks on leg bones can show that a person was into horseback riding. You can tell almost anything by examining the skeleton even though the person has been dead for months. Even years. Because bones keep."

"Why are we having this wonderful conversation?"

Rick noticed that he'd had an erection while viewing his adorable wife but that it was petering out. This meant that if they continued talking about skeletons he would upchuck on the rug. His personal analysis of his erotic/chemical biology was having a depressing effect on him. He liked to think of himself as a pretty healthy person, who sometimes had aches and pains due to the Nautilus machines at the Club. But Rick really didn't want to know too much about the workings of his inner body until the age when he had to face the fact that mortality was a reality. But, living with Rosie, especially when they were researching one of their books, was always difficult for Rick because Rosie seemed to glow as she uttered all sorts of gruesome facts with her gorgeous heavily painted lips.

"Well, they identified Baby Sue because her jawbone was cracked in several places and so they contacted dentists to find a match. That's how they found the x-rays of her teeth. She'd visited a dentist when her jawbone had been broken. Probably, somebody hit her badly."

"Poor kid."

"You see, Rick, we've got to understand the underground energy of this punk, New Wave, hard core crowd who feels pain is erotic so we can hunt down whomever is responsible for Baby Sue's terrible death."

Rosie paused for a second while applying silver eye shadow above her brilliant emerald eyes. The color effect turned Rosie into a creature from another planet because the light from her eyes was intensely fierce.

"You know I don't have the stomach for pain and skeletons and that sort of thing," Rick complained.

"You must have. You keep finding things like severed hands and mutilated bodies. It must be in your karma."

"How can I get it out of my karma?"

"By working it through and purifying your unconscious. That's what the other book did, didn't it? And now the movie is the catharsis for the severed-hands murder. Don't you see?"

Her voice cooed in a singsong motherly tone.

"You don't dream of hands anymore, do you?"

Rick did. But he didn't want to admit it because he was afraid Rosie would form another philosophical hypothesis which would be too gruesome. He'd gotten to the place where he could live with his severed-hands dreams. He was used to them. In fact, sometimes he missed them. After finding the first severed hand on West Broadway, spotting the other one on the Carlos canvas, then capturing the murderer of the bodies which belonged to the severed hands, these hands were definitely a part of Rick's personality and his life experience. So what if he woke up sweaty and screaming in the middle of the night, dreaming of those hands? Rosie woke up too, and made passionate love to him so he could forget his fear. That wasn't bad, was it?

What Rick was really worried about was whether the severed-hands dreams would be replaced. Last night, he could swear he dreamt of a young breastless girl being whipped by a dark Spanish general wearing medals of honor from his country. Was this the beginning of a new breasts nightmare? Would this go on until he found the murderer of Baby Sue? If so, he'd better hustle.

"Are you ready to leave, sweetheart?"

"The other thing, Rick . . ." Rosie said as she practiced being a ravishing version of a "Dynasty" bitch, but was having trouble because her sweet smile could never be as sardonic as was necessary for prime-time television, ". . . the other thing is that I've been doing research on random killers."

"What are random killers?" Rick asked, twirling her about and kissing her soundly on her apple-red lips.

"Did you smear my lipstick?"

"Absolutely."

"Good," she laughed, then toppled over into his lap. Rick thought, what would happen when they appeared at the Snake Club? This outfit was Rosie's idea. Rick would rather have dressed in old fashioned sadomasochistic leather but Rosie had said no, that was out of fashion and they had to go there as swells so that they would start a new trend. Rick replied that the last time a word like swells was used was in a Noel Coward play. But Rosie said it was the right time to re-create the language of panache and that the new woman and the new man were now known as the modern girl and modern boy.

Rosie answered Rick's question about random killers.

"Random killers are people who pick up anyone and kill them right off with no reason," she explained.

"That's gruesome."

"What's really gruesome is that they're all men," she said with subtle feminist satisfaction.

"Maybe like everything else, women will catch up to them."

"I don't think so. Women are more personal. That's not the way these random killers kill. One said there wasn't anyway in which he hadn't killed. He had crucified some victims. Filleted some others like fish. The victims are mostly young women but sometimes they can be young men. It seems, Rick, that somehow these random killers get sex and killing confused. One man actually said, when he was caught, that if he was sexually attracted to a girl he had to kill her before he could kiss her."

"I'm getting ill."

"The theory is," Rosie continued, "do you want a wet cloth? No. You okay? Good. The theory is that the selection of and talking to the victim is the foreplay of the erotic act. The killing is the orgasm. You know how that goes."

"No, I don't."

"Well, the killing is the penetration, putting the knife or bullet into the victim. Then, after the victim dies, there's a sense of relief, an orgasm of sorts. And the police have found that most victims are physically abused, sexually and otherwise, and that money or jewelry is never taken. Isn't that interesting?"

"Ugh."

"Rick, these killers are untreatable so they're usually put into a hospital situation. They're good actors so they pretend to be rehabilitated and get paroled. They're on the streets right this minute. Kushel is compiling a list of some in the city. One of them might have killed our girl."

"Our girl?"

"Yes, Baby Sue."

"I doubt it. What about the pimp's death?"

She ignored his question and continued talking. "The reason I brought this up is that the experts have found that most of them were deprived during childhood, that they were abused and molested, and they continue this practice on their victims. Isn't that sad?"

"I can't stand much more of this."

"Another interesting thing is that some of them are sons of prostitutes. But they're hard to find because they lead very sane lives. Lots of them are clerks. It's not like the Mafia. I mean, you can spot the beasts. They're obvious."

"Let's leave?"

"Wait a minute, let's try to work out some kind of scenario."

"What scenario? The minute we walk into the Snake Club with these duds, we're going to be tapped as suckers."

"Rick, nobody uses that word. Please don't use antiquated language or we'll be considered outsiders."

Rick scratched his head.

"Maybe we shouldn't go."

"Don't worry. Kushel will be watching over us."

"Mario hates that Lithuanian cop."

"But Dad doesn't know about this. Besides, Dad is still not talking to me. Kushel made me swear that I wouldn't go to the Snake Club without backup."

"What about me?"

"You're a wonderfully strong black belt and you saved my life, but Kushel says we've got to have cops around."

"But we don't have to go along with him. We're not the police."

"I know. But Kushel suspects us since we made all that money on the severed-hands murder. Come on, Rick, we've got to get to work."

Downstairs, the cab driver spoke no English so Rick had to draw a map to get them from Broadway and Houston to East Second Street and First Avenue. All the way down, Rosie babbled on about their duty to the establishment of morality and sanity in the American culture. But of course, she added, they had to do their duty, Italian style, which meant that, like the Romans, they had to be courageous and fierce. Rosie simply adored the Romans.

"You know, it's funny, Rick. I've always had to be a loner to grow. I've never been a groupie."

"What do you mean?"

"Well, if my loyalty had been to the Italians instead of the human race, I would never have been able to write *The Severed Hands*."

"Huh?"

"I mean, if my loyalty was only to the Italians, I would have censored everything, you see what I mean?"

"You are Italian. You will always be Italian. You are the most Italian person I know."

"Not true. My family is."

"Not so. They only seem to be more Italian. It's a put-on. They're really American. They like electronic toasters, washing machines, video machines, and wall-to-wall carpets. You don't. You're the real thing. You don't fit into this culture at all. You're an eccentric wonderful person and I love you."

"Dear Rick. You aren't threatened by eccentrics like most people."

"That's because the New England Wasp gentility are crazier than anyone. Take Aunt Mandy, for instance. When she was growing up, her mother, my grandmother, spent all her time sculpting animals on the great lawn. Her lawn became very famous. People came from all over the world to see it. They ignored the Second World War and other world problems and traveled to Connecticut to see her grass animals. My God. When I grew up, I had a private zoo."

"I love animals," she agreed.

"But these weren't animals, they were grass bushes. Everything was artificial. My grandmother thought she was very civic minded so she gave every poor family in town proper shoes. Grandmother believed that if people went shoeless it did something to their morals. So, they had shoes. And, on every holiday, she prepared lavish picnic baskets to be delivered to the poor. I remember one maid, Nellie, telling me how she hated holidays because she had to deliver Gran's baskets. Funny, isn't it, how the poor hate the poor."

"And the middle class hate the middle class."

"I never remember a middle class in Connecticut. It was only our crowd and the poor."

"Well, the poor and the rich are the only people worth knowing. They're wholly eccentric and they're permitted to be."

"And the crew we're going to visit now?"

"They're misfits, like us. They're the artists, the avant-garde, the leaders of style. They struggle to serve their fantasies. One or two of them become media-hyped and become famous, usually through music or painting. Then they take over the culture of the world. The poor never know about them because they don't have the time to stay out all night. The rich are titillated by them. And we, my dear, must understand them. Because if some of them are going around murdering children, we have to know why."

Rosie kissed Rick as the driver, Mr. Sanchez, stopped abruptly in front of the Snake Club. The entire street looked as if it had been bombed out. Amidst the rubble were city animals, some human. Rick shivered as he paid the driver and led Rosie into this den of erotica, wondering where Kushel's tribe were, and whether they could be counted on in a pinch.

At the Club's entrance, the long bar was inundated with underground types. Rick was glad he had been prepared for this by watching MTV; this crowd did not threaten him. The first group was wearing various versions of the Apache hairstyle. Some heads were partially shaved. Some were entirely shaved. But whatever hair was there stood up straight, lacquered by various new products for this look. Several women had shaved heads in front and long tails of hair in the rear. Some men had long, curly locks. Rick was sad to see that the New Wave crew cut was out of fashion. Most men and women wore the same type of strawberry-red lipstick. A group was wearing the newest fashion of plastic grab bag clothes, trimmed with tin foil. These clothes were very practical because when they got dirty they could be used to wrap leftovers.

Rosie and Rick walked the length of the bar to a large, long room where people were standing around watching a woman/man in the center of a small stage. The he/she was singing that she/he was a monkey/creature/person. Then the monkey/creature/person took out a horn, tooted on it and screeched that cats were his/her primary way to have orgasm.

"Gross," Rosie whispered. A huge Fat Man, dressed in a white suit with blue sequin stars was coming their way.

"Sidney Greenstreet, *Maltese Falcon*, nineteen forty-one," Rick whispered into Rosie's ear.

"No, its *Three Strangers*. Nineteen forty-three to Nineteen forty-four."

"Hello. I was told the media was coming down tonight," the Fat Man said, saliva dripping into his moustached overlip. "I've set up a table for you. A special table."

"Don't bother."

"It's up there. Come on."

He pointed to a Romeo-Juliet type balcony that seemed to be built out of nowhere. Two huge men were standing over the space, dressed as guards of a sheik's harem. They stood with arms crossed and wore long sabres. Their bodies were oiled and shaved of hair.

"Is this necessary?" Rick asked, pointing to the armament.

"Sometimes we all need to be physically violent. Most times we are sensible and use violence on our senses, the mind, and the erotic parts," he sangsong his words in a manner common to this underground, as if all words were part of a song, patches here, patches there.

"I'd rather stay with the crowd," Rosie said, smoothing back her hair under her tiny hat spiked with feathers and rhinestones.

"Here," the Fat Man said, waving aside dozens of patrons to clear a space where another table was put. "Sit here."

Rosie and Rick sat amidst the patrons who were mostly dressed in black, the only touches of bright color were body tattoos and hair dye.

One modern girl had painted her cheeks with red blush and added green highlights. Another had painted her lips like Joan Crawford. Another looked like a French schoolgirl, complete with bows in her hair. Shades of Proust, Rick thought. Next to him, a woman and a man were wearing matching tuxedos. The tuxedos were odd. The tops were shredded crepe draped around their chests in toga fashion. Then, there was a swirl of cutaway which began but never ended. Instead, the trousers were slashed to show flesh. The man and woman were identically dressed, down to the last detail of makeup, only one had breasts and the other didn't.

"Outrageous," Rosie whispered but she was as fascinated as Rick was.

Two women in large black satin jackets, rhinestone ties and rhinestone headbands on their hats, walked by the table. Suddenly, they dropped their jackets. Underneath they wore only rhinestones, one for the tip of each breast.

"I have a dirty mind," Rick whispered.

"I can see why. This is really acting out fantasies. I can see how anything goes here, whatever you want to be, you can be.

"Even a murderer," Rick said grimly.

"Look, Rick, what a wonderful looking girl."

In the center of the stage was a blue-haired girl, clothed in a maze of white dotted swiss. Some of the costume was tattered and dirty and some of it was sparkling white. The dotted swiss was accessorized by a headpiece of white ostrich feathers over a plastic space helmut. Under the dotted swiss, the girl wore silk bloomers embroidered with red satin hearts. Through a slit in the gauze, her white gloved hand appeared, holding a corsage of helium balloons. In her other hand she held one white lily.

"She's wonderful," Rosie whispered.

The girl began swaying, her tiny satin booties shining on the dirt and grime of the center stage.

"I've been a honcho, a hero, a hustler, a hooker and now, I'm a goddess," she sang, tapping the heads of the audience with her lily. "I'm a nice Catholic girl from Rockaway, Queens, and I'm everything daddy wanted me to be."

The crowd laughed.

"My daddy taught me all those naughty things and he taught me how to like them. And now I'm teaching my daddy how grown up I can be," she sang. "I'm punishing my daddy. You understand what I mean?"

The crowd swelled and roared.

"Yes, Ice Goddess," they screamed in unison.

"I wonder if she wrote those lyrics," Rosie asked.

"Why do you ask?"

"Because they fit into our case. You know, child abuse by fathers."

"Let's listen for clues."

"Now, I'm what everybody wants to be," the girl said. "I'm daddy's little girl."

Slowly, she took off the dotted swiss environment and stood there, her white rhinestones outlining the rose tips of her young budding breasts, the bloomers giving her an old-fashioned Bloomsbury look, her little satin slippers showering her with young innocence. Then she released the helium balloons and the crowd surged to capture them.

The girl laughed at the crowd. Waving her hips, she walked off the stage. Suddenly, she stopped. Then, looking straight at Rick, she handed him the lily.

13

"*You uptown types* are boring," Ice said nastily, her steely black eyes not budging from Rick's face. Rick flinched as the young angel/devil demoted them to tourists and amidst these young modern girls and boys, Rosie and he seemed ancient.

The air was filled with smoke blasts and unmentionable smells. A trio of boys played droning clusters of notes, using chiming bells and abrasive buzz saws. The sound created an electronic jangle that had a weird resonance. The boys and girls in the audience responded in that way too; several were kneeling before the group as if they were in church.

On a large screen random imagery was projected by the three young boys, creating an atmospheric style that was truly original. After twenty minutes of this enormous display of energy, blackness covered the stage and they disappeared. Recorded music took over as, one by one, the audience rose to their feet, their reverence ended.

Several people were running around with cameras, taking shots of the audience.

"We'll probably be in the *New York Post* tomorrow," Rosie complained.

"This is a free zone. Anybody can do anything here," Ice said contemptuously.

"It seems more like a battle zone," Rosie quipped.
"Which war?"
Rick noticed Rosie's tone was brittle.
"It's play-make-believe time for us. We don't do career here. We try things out and nothing is recorded. There are no poets or writers. Only *People* magazine."
"We're writers," Rosie said defensively.
"That's what I mean. There are no writers," Ice responded.
Rick interrupted the growing hostility between these two.
"There are painters and filmmakers and photographers," he said, pointing to those scurrying about.
"A few," Ice agreed. "They're the manipulators. The ones who make the money. We live this chaos. They package it."
"What's the chaos about?" Rick asked gently.
"It's everybody's last stop. Most kids have been burnt out in high school. They've come here to bury the body."
Her answer saddened Rick but there was a sense of the apocalypse in the club. Its texture reminded Rick of the *Blue Angel*, his favorite German film, starring Marlene Dietrich. He watched the kids swerving and brushing against each other but not touching, conveying a sense that they had no future, and only a terrible past to remember. He knew, because of their age, that this crew was the TV generation. Most of them had spent their childhood in front of the tube where TV game shows were a favorite metaphor. Not aware of the written word, hardly aware of the visual breadth of painting, this crew could barely concentrate on a movie. Yet, they loved the golden oldies because the films gave them a sense of family and history they did not seem to have in their personal lives.
Rick concentrated on the dancers' movements. In the blackness there was a sterility which was new to him. This was not like the pre-Berlin days where there was enormous sexual tension. Perhaps he was wrong. He viewed the group carefully, analyzing the differences in the crowd.

There was the hard core crew, dressed in leather, silver accessories, crosses and swastikas, proclaiming their violent heterosexual tastes. Then the New Wave kids with their softer clothes and crew cuts who conveyed the androgynous look. Now, a new group, the little modern girls and boys like Ice who seemed neither androgynous nor heterosexual but fell somewhere in between.

Shivering at this concept, Rick moved closer to Rosie, kissed her cheek and held her hand. Ice noticed his gesture.

"I'm magic," she stated. A girl walked by, nude to the waist. As she passed the table, a young man followed, painting her back with sparkling blue paint.

"Don't know about your fancy clothes and your rhinestone hair," Ice singsang.

"Ice. We're here for a reason," Rosie said, attempting to be friendly to the girl.

"Can it. I thought your guy was cute but I'm afraid you're both history."

"So soon?" Rosie joked, trying a new tack.

"Don't patronize me."

Rick squirmed. Two females attacking each other was not a comfortable thing to watch, especially when one was his wife. But he waited, knowing Rosie must have a plan.

"Do you let your lady walk all over you?" Ice addressed this question to Rick.

"Ice. We need answers," he said.

Ice laughed. Taking the lily from the table top, she tossed it onto the messy floor to be trampled on by a crew of sadomasochistic religious freaks who were doing a strange group dance. All male, they were banging into each other, holding on to lavish silver crosses.

"Slam dancing," Ice explained, seeing Rick's puzzled look. As he watched the lily destroyed he felt depressed, sure Ice's gesture was symbolic. This young girl was like no one he'd ever met. She was hot, passionate, but all ice.

"Look, if you don't talk to us, you're going to have to speak to the police," Rosie cautioned.

At the mention of police, Rick caught fear in Ice's eyes.

"So why not talk to us," Rosie continued, "we're only writers."

Ice caved in.

"Did you know Baby Sue?" Rosie questioned.

"She worked here but I didn't know her."

"Are you aware that she's been killed?"

"I heard."

"Do you have any theories about why she was murdered?"

"Yup. She was a cuff and whip lady. Those guys are mean. You have to be strong to survive them."

Rosie watched Ice carefully. Rick could see that his wife was turning on her inner tape recorder because a real recorder would not work with the blasting music. Watching, Rick suddenly felt protective of Ice. There was something tragically innocent about her, though she spoke like an experienced hustler. He felt she needed someone to care for her, that she was a badly marked child, in grownup clothes.

"You're going to need friends, Ice. The Fat Man described you as his main star. But I'll bet you're underage, aren't you?"

Ice flinched. Rosie had done it again.

"Just like that."

"Just like what?"

"You want me to blab or you'll turn me into the cops. Just like that."

"Not us. We don't like cops," Rick interjected but Rosie shot him a keep-quiet look.

"Okay. What do you want to know? Baby Sue was selling herself on the cuff and whip market for her pimp, Hoofer Harris. But Hoofer Harris has died and gone to heaven, or so I've been told. That's alright. They'll be twelve others to take his place. Only Baby Sue won't be working."

"Is this common?"

"Cuffs and whips? Every girl on the street knows about them. Look at those creeps." Ice pointed to the black leather crowd. "See the way they're banging into each other. Violence is the only thing they believe in." She sangsong every word. "Because it's real. You can touch it. You can feel it."

"Is that your scene?" Rosie pursued.

Ice turned frosty.

"I don't have a scene. Nobody can figure me out. I play it moment to moment." Suddenly the music stopped and a spotlight shined on Ice.

"When I was nine, my daddy started me and then all my other daddies loved me so," she sang to the crowd.

People watched with gleaming glows on their faces that could only be induced by drugs.

"Then I had one daddy for money. And one for a car and duds."

The spot returned to the floor as the music blasted again and people began moving.

"What about love, Ice?" Rosie asked.

"What about love?" She threw back her head and laughed. "You know how I can tell a sucker? They always dress the same. They always look the same. They always say hello. Like you," she accused them. "Well, when they say hello right off, I mean, that's when you know you can take them." She paused. "And the other thing they always talk about is love. You're suckers," she accused.

"And you?" Rosie asked angrily.

"I'm a cunt."

"Cunt is a word isolating the sexual organ of a woman in an impersonal crude way," Rosie explained.

"Downtown, a cunt is a girl who knows what's she's doing. We have cunts here. Then we have hard core." She pointed to the floor. "And then we have modern girls. Everyone else, people like you, are suckers. Weirdos. Tourists."

"It might be someone like that that we're looking for," Rick interjected calmly.

"Baby Sue was into getting hurt. You know what that means?"

She glared at Rosie with her steely black eyes. Rosie's

emerald eyes glinted in response. Rick panicked. His chest heaved. He wondered whether Rosie and Ice were going to have a fistfight and what he would have to do to stop it. He looked around the room, hoping to see a friendly face, but saw no one he could even identify as a human being.

"Baby Sue ran with an Elephant Man. He was over three hundred pounds. I asked her once, what are you doing with this guy and she said sometimes when it was cold and she didn't feel like walking the streets he'd give her money so she could pay Hoofer off."

"Do you know who he is?"

"I heard he left for the West Coast when her body was found. But I don't think he could hurt anyone. He was strictly a masochist. *He* liked to get hurt."

"How did you get into this world?" Rick asked hastily.

"My mother sent me here, first-class mail," her lips pouted. "She didn't want me. She never liked me so I left home and I learned not to kiss ass for nobody. So I sing. And I live. That's what I do. I am my own woman. Cunt Number One."

"Lighten up," Rosie snarled, her rhinestone hat bobbing in a threatening way.

"You lighten up. You and your man here are in my territory now."

The spotlight came on again and the crowd again pressed around Ice, their glazed eyes drinking in her existence. There was something magical about her which Rick felt he had to be a part of, but the thought frightened him.

"Will you help us?" Rosie asked gently.

"What is your pleasure?" Ice sangsong.

"We're trying to find out more about Baby Sue. We're trying to find out who her murderer might be. We think it's connected to a flock of young girls' murders. Won't you help?"

"Don't think so."

"Don't you care?"

"Nope. I only care about Ice."

"But . . ."

"Don't lecture me. People die here and nobody cares. There's a virus here. And it's spreading. We're all heading for death. Read about us in the *Post*," she laughed.

"So, it's no?" Rick reiterated.

"Yeah, it's no no no," Ice said briskly. Then in a speedy movement, she left in a huff.

"Well, I guess that didn't work," Rosie said.

"You two were really bitching it up."

"I'm ashamed of myself. She's only a kid. But she has an irritating way of flaunting everything, especially her hots for you."

Rick avoided the obvious.

"Let's get out of here," he said.

On their way out, Rick spotted a face he knew. It was Arnoldo, their top-floor neighbor who lived with the Prince robot, and other electronic gadgets. Here, at the Snake Club, Arnoldo was outfitted with black leather, spike wristlets, chains, silver jewelry, three swastikas and a severed cross in his ear. When he spotted Rick, Arnoldo ran out the door and disappeared.

"What on earth?" Rosie gasped, running after him.

"Hey, Arnoldo," Rick called out.

Outside the Club, Arnoldo stopped, a sullen look on his face.

"What are you two doing here?" he asked. "This is my club. It's mine."

"You got it," Rosie chimed in.

"We're researching a murder," Rick explained.

"Not another one. Rick, I can't take it. Last time, the Princess, who is now the Prince, almost broke down completely after someone tried to kill Rosie. Are we going to have another one? If so, tell me. I'll protect Rosie electronically. Maybe I'll put a bug between her breasts that she can press if someone attacks her. How about it, Rosie?"

"You leave my breasts alone."

"They didn't leave that poor girl's breasts alone."

"So, you do know about that," Rick said.

"Gossip runs rampant in SoHo. Everybody is wondering why you seem to have all the luck."

"Luck?"

"Finding bodies and that kind of thing. It happens to nobody else. You make all the money. Fate is smiling at you," Arnoldo laughed.

"Arnoldo, stop avoiding our question," Rosie scolded. "What are you doing here, dressed like that?"

"Taxi," Arnoldo shouted as a cab passed by. "Let's get away from here. It's not good for me to be seen with swells."

"How do you usually get home?"

"I walk but then, I'm dressed for it," his chest swelled under his leather.

"Cab," Rosie called out. Suddenly one stopped. When they were in the cab, the driver stared, shaking his head at the strangely dressed trio.

"Broadway and Houston, please," Rick told the driver. Then to Arnoldo, "How long have you been doing this?"

"Well, it happened when I saw Mel Gibson as Mad Max. Then I saw *Blade Runner* and knew what I had to do. You see, ever since I got into electronics, I've been lonely. Electronics changes one's entire perspective on life. You can get anything you want by simply pressing a button. Someday soon, we'll have mental telepathy and we won't even need buttons. So, I found that I needed an easy way to relax. The usual path to sex is long. You have to meet a girl. Ask her out. Buy her flowers. Write poetry to her. Oh, here we are. Home and hearth."

The cab screeched to a stop in front of their loft building. Rosie paid the cab fare. Rick helped Arnoldo out of the cab. In his leather outfit, Arnoldo was stiffer than usual. They unlocked the front door and crammed into the elevator. Arnoldo put the elevator on computer energy transport so that they were forced to stop at his loft first. When the elevator door opened, the Prince was waiting. When he spotted Rosie, he made loving sounds for his beloved.

"Chuggg uglgug luggg," Prince murmured. Then he walked to her side, raised his electronic arm and touched her.

"He's cold," Rosie complained, hugging Rick.

"He loves you," Arnoldo's big brown eyes looked adoringly at Rosie.

"I love you, too," Rick said. "Hey, let's sit down. You know the Prince will chuggalug for hours. Can you turn him off."

"Oh, must we?" Arnoldo complained.

"Tell us about the Snake Club?" Rosie asked, when they were snuggled on Arnoldo's electronic rumble couch and the Prince was temporarily quiet.

"Well, as I said before, working with electronics all day, it's hard to make the transition to being human. I found out at the Snake Club, all you have to wear is something announcing your sexual preference and, bingo! Because I'm a heterosexual, I wear leather. The leather girls come on to me without my having to do anything. It's easy. If you're into groups, you wear Boy George duds. If you're a modern boy, you wear plastic bags. And if you're into trios, you dress like your favorite planet. It's wonderful. Nobody has to say a thing. All you do is dress right."

"I thought sex was on its way out at the Snake Club," Rick noted.

"It's not the kind of sex you would know about," Arnoldo said shyly. "It's different. Nobody cares. It's not heavy."

"Arnoldo, does it make you happy?" Rosie asked with concern.

"Happy? Who wants to be happy? I just want to stay alive," he answered.

14

"Mrs. Ramsey. It's Lieutenant Kushel," the voice over the phone said. "I'm here to talk to you about the murder of Baby Sue. Can you let me in?"

Rosie had the phone pressed to her ear while she was kissing Rick's body. Naked and sweaty, they'd been making love for hours. Rick was lying back, relishing Rosie's kisses, hoping the outside world would stop revolving so they could be caught in this moment of time. When the phone rang, Rick pleaded with Rosie not to answer it. Always efficient, she had.

"Ohhhhh," she screamed into Rick's ear, causing him to jump up in bed.

"What is it?"

"Kushel. He's downstairs. What should we do?"

"I guess we have to see him now that you've answered the phone. Silly, that's why we have an answering machine. So that we don't have to be interrupted."

"That's for work."

"Uhhh. It's for private moments too," he said, pointing to his erection which he was jamming into a blue Adidas jogging suit.

Rick took the phone from Rosie.

"Hi, Kush."

"Is that you, Mr. Ramsey? I was talking to your wife. Is she there? I want both of you to be there."

"We're here."

"Good. Would you let me in?"

"I can't. You see, we don't have a bell. I have to come down for you."

"Send down the Prince. That'll give Kushel a thrill," Rosie called from the inner sanctum of their large red bathroom.

Because she was an Aries, Rosie loved the color red, the color of Aries. Their red bathroom was one of the reasons Rick upchucked on the living room rug instead of the john where the vibrant color always added to whatever misery Rick felt.

It was a red world in the bathroom. Red toothbrushes. Red shower curtain. Red frames on the prints and even on the Mona Lisa, Rosie's favorite bathroom meditation. There were red towels. Even red toilet paper. (Rosie would not reveal where she found red toilet paper). The pièce de résistance was a red toilet seat in the shape of a heart which read: Rick and Rosie, always in love. What a thing to sit on!

Visitors hardly ever used these private facilities, for there was a smaller bathroom off the living room that was decorated in white with yellow daisies for guests' peace of mind. When there was an emergency because the smaller facilities were occupied, a guest would be allowed in this inner sanctum. The first sound heard was Ahhhhugghhhhh. Even Aunt Irene, who was fond of loud colors in her constant state of pre–World War II costume, shouted Ahhhhugghhhhh. On the other hand, Aunt Mandy, upon viewing the place, had simply toppled over in a dead faint, straightaway.

The reason for their shock was there was no preparation for the red. The large bedroom with the skylight framing the twin towers of Lower Manhattan (a view most people would kill for) was decorated in a soft mauve-lavender motif because Rosie's ascendant was Pisces. Thank God for that or Rick would never get any sleep. If her ascendant was Aries, their bedroom would have been bloody red, too.

Their bedroom was painted lavender and filled with the antique gold furniture painted by Arnoldo's one and only friend, the artist, Patric Murnahan.

Patric was now famous. When Rosie and Rick had moved into the loft, he was a down-and-out person who needed money, so he'd painted the bedroom furniture. The set was worth lots of money now because Patric, being an egoist as most painters really are despite their shabby looks, had signed every piece. Thus their bedroom was worth a great deal of money. This did not take into account the dining-room area, which Patric had also decorated with his talented hands.

Rosie had added to Patric's decor with couches and chairs of soft shades of purple. Whenever Rick walked into their bedroom he felt like a Roman emperor and pretended Rosie was the lead priestess in his harem or whatever the Romans called their sex clubs.

At sunset, even nature cooperated because sunsets enhanced the bedroom with a lovely purple rainbow which reflected an eerie spacey light over everything.

While Rosie's astrological sun sign and ascendancy dominated the bedroom and bathroom, her moon sign dominated the remainder of the loft. Her moon sign being Leo, the golden colors of the Lion, yellow and orange, were everywhere, sometimes mixed with soft purples and bright red, which Rosie said reflected all of her stars.

Rick was happy that Carl Jung was right in his thesis that the perfect marriage was when a man's sun sign matched his lady's moon sign; for Rick was a Leo and this meant he and Rosie would love each other forever.

Now Rosie exited from the red bathroom in a lavender jogging suit with a lavender bow in her dark curls.

"You look adorable."

She kissed him.

"I'll tell the Prince to get Kushel."

Rick dialed Arnoldo's number for the Prince. Also, he

wanted to reassure their top-floor neighbor that they still liked him although he was into leather, crosses, and handcuffs.

"Arnoldo?"
"Are you mad at me, Rick?"
"Why should I be mad at you?"
"Because of last night."
"Each to his own."
Arnoldo's voice trembled.
"Is she mad?"
"Don't think so."
"Do you know that definitely?"
"Never do."
"I know. She's exciting, isn't she?"
Arnoldo's voice always flipflopped in his adoration of Rosie.
"Hey, buddy. Could you send the Prince down to the door. That crazy detective is here and Rosie wants to scare him."
"I'll ask the Prince if he wants to do that."
Rick heard the Prince's chuggulugg.
"Prince says he doesn't like cops. Why don't I simply put the elevator on the computer energy transport? That'll blow the guy's mind."
"Okay."
Rosie waited for the answer.
"The Prince said no to cops. Arnoldo is sending the computer down for Kushel."
Several minutes later they heard grunting as the elevator sped past their floor to the top, then the elevator groaned as it went down to the fifth, then past their floor again, down to the second, then finally up to their floor.
"Arnoldo is sending Kushel on a trip," Rick laughed.
When he opened the elevator door, Kushel stood there, looking pea green. Still in his Sherlock Holmes phase, as he had been during the hands caper, Kushel wore the full Holmes regalia, though it was summer. Last year, Kushel smoked a

pipe and wore a tweed hat. Due to his new found fame and success because of the solving of the Mafia rooftop murder (the hands caper), Kushel wore a Burberry coat and matching hat, the kind Sherlock Holmes always wore in the films with Basil Rathbone.

"What is this? 'Star Trek'?"

"Kush. I'm sorry about the elevator. It often has a mind of its own."

"The place is eccentric," Rosie added.

"Eccentric? It's downright lethal!"

"Want a Coke?" she asked.

"Uggghhhh."

"Are you going to throw up," she demanded. "If you are, please go into the bathroom."

"Let me sit a minute."

Kushel sat in Woolfe's Lair, throwing a curious look about, examining the Bloomsbury couches and chairs. He didn't remove his hat or coat and looked odd, sitting there. Rick noted that the English Holmes did not match with the English Woolfe.

Rick sat on a Casablanca chair, twirling his legs around it like Bogie always did. Rosie, taking his cue, raced over to the grand piano and played a refrain from "As Time Goes By."

"What is that song?" Kushel's eyes popped.

Though Kushel was a Lithuanian boy from Brooklyn, he had no knowledge of important things like films. He didn't even know who Dirty Harry was.

"Are you here for a special reason?" Rosie yanked herself from the piano with such speed that Rick knew she wasn't feeling happy anymore.

"In a minute," Kushel pleaded, still breathing heavily under his Holmes wrap.

"Croissant. Coffee. Tea." she offered.

"Coke. It's bad for my teeth but when I feel topsy-turvy, it's wonderful," Kushel uttered.

Rosie, a Coke addict, gave him a dirty look. The reason Rosie drank Coke all the time was that her energy was on massive speed while the rest of the human race was on mundane, being concerned with sordid things like how to get through the day safely.

"Here you are," she handed Kushel a Coke in a blue champagne glass that had been a wedding gift from one of the numerous Caesare cousins.

Slowly, the detective sipped the sweet bubbly. After a while, he seemed to return to this life. When Kushel removed his hat, Rick saw that Kushel's hair was thinning.

Slowly, Kushel looked around the loft. His eyes popped at the Indian ram statues which led the path into Woolfe's Lair. He stared at the grand piano, bright white with a dark red rug on the seat for comfort. Above him was a sterling silver airplane mobile by Arnoldo, posed for takeoff from the high ceilings. The Man, a bronze sculpture by Patric in his neo-Nazi phase, stood watch over the piano. Whalebone sculptures from Africa and an African dance mask hung on two walls. The room was a crazy mismatch and gave the loft an intercontinental flavor which Rick loved.

"What kind of a place is this?" Kushel complained. "I feel like I'm on a ship."

"It's the ship of life. Changing. Moving," Rosie said, standing over him in an intimidating manner.

"Look, Mrs. Ramsey. I came here to help you out."

"That's nice of you, Kush," Rick said.

"What do you want?" Rosie demanded, operating on her father's edict that cops were to be treated like the beasts.

"Don't be like your dad. I'm not here to hurt you."

Kushel trembled at the mention of Mario. Rick could see that Mario had really gotten to the detective. Before he met Mario, Kushel had been an ordinary brutal cop. Now he was fearful, due to Mario's constant pruning of his ego.

"Look, we ran into this vice case. There were things that were interesting, so I thought I'd come down and give you a few hints as to how we're thinking."

"Terrible English," Rosie said, in her continuing harassment of the detective.

Kushel flinched.

"I learned English at night school. I'm not rich, like other people," he retorted.

"Your English is fine, Kush," Rick said, giving Rosie the lay-off-this-dick sign. After all, Kushel was there to help them in her favorite new project: their next: the breasts affair.

"Well, we had this crazy woman in prison," Kushel began. "She liked prison. Said she'd never been happier. She was there on a vice charge. While working for an uptown madam she set fire to a customer. So the madam was on the outs with her and wouldn't bail her out. Anyhow, she told the prison warden she heard voices. We thought she was trying to cop an insanity plea but she really loved the prison. When she said they were kids' voices and that they were demons and that she had them in a movie, the warden became interested. Anyway, he called vice and the vice people went down and she told them she had a certain movie stashed. It seems certain clients liked to watch this movie while sampling the pleasures of her flesh. Anyhow, the vice guys picked up the film and when they viewed it, they told us about it."

"Why?"

"Because one of the kids who was acting in this dirty movie was Baby Sue."

"Oh boy," Rosie swore.

"The movie was filthy. They had a kid play a girl getting punished by her daddy. And they had boys and girls doing—I can't say it—I've been having bad dreams ever since I saw that filth."

"Did the woman say where she got the film?"

As usual, Rosie kept her cool in the face of upsetting research.

"She said these movies are plentiful. Anyone can buy them. She said there's a ring of kid stuff. Books. Movies. Photos. Stuff like that."

"How about the real thing?"

"She said she heard stories that kids are for sale but most

madams won't go for it. Her notion was that it's probably run by a group of sick pimps. I don't understand it at all." He shook his egg-shaped head. "The resident shrink at headquarters says that some men aren't capable of love so kids seem safe to them. Am I crazy or is this really happening?"

Rick felt bad for Kushel. Even experienced detectives couldn't hack this kid stuff.

Rosie sat next to the man.

"Do you have children?" she asked kindly.

"Three girls and one boy. They're only kids. But they're the same age as the kids in that movie."

"It's terrible," Rosie agreed. "We've got to find out about this ring. They must be getting girls and boys from somewhere."

"Mostly runaways."

"What about the day-care centers? Those stories about child abuse?" Rick suggested.

Rosie shook her head.

"No. This ring teaches kids how to act sexually, which means they must have somewhere where kids can be trained."

"Rosie?"

"Sorry, Rick. I know this is hard to take. But we've got to stay tough. If we fold now, we won't be able to get to the bottom of this awful mess."

Tessa cried hysterically as the man held on to her. She'd disobeyed Ice and sneaked into the Snake Club to see her sister perform. Ten minutes later, a dark-haired man asked how old she was.

"Eighteen," Tessa lied.

"Identification please?"

"What's happening here?" the Fat Man asked, recognizing the man as a vice detective.

"You're letting minors into this place. You're in bad trouble."

"This kid sneaked in."

"You'll be hearing from us. Come on, kid."
"Tell Ice," Tessa pleaded. "I'm her sister."

Tessa was at the East Fifth Street Police Station only an hour, when Ice appeared, still in her performance clothes. The desk sergeant laughed at her appearance.

"My sister is here."
"Name?"
"Tessa Martin."
"She's in the back."
"Can I see her?"
"In a minute. How old are you?"
"Eighteen."
"Identification?"
"I have none on me. I ran over from the Snake Club. I work there."
"We'll check you out. What about your sister?"
"What about her?"
"Where's your family?"
"I'm the only family she has," Ice lied.
"How old is she?"
"Fifteen."
"Well, we'll have to wait until family court decides what to do with her. Usually, they send the kids to foster families."
"But I can take care of her."
"Sorry. Maybe if you were an upstanding citizen."

He laughed at her outfit again.

"Can I see her now?"
"Down the hall. First door to the left."

Ice trembled as she walked down the long hall. When she walked into the room, Tessa was sitting, quietly sobbing. When she saw Ice, she bolted to her sister's side.

"I told you not to go outside the house," Ice scolded.
"I wanted to hear you sing."
"Well, well, you've got us into trouble. I've got to get a lawyer to help us. No more foster families for us."
"What are we going to do?" Tessa wailed.

"Don't you worry. I'll get us taken care of. But don't tell them about Linda. I said we had no family. Understand?"

"Yes."

"Be brave. Ice will take care of things."

When she left the police station, Ice walked fast. Though she was dressed like garbage, no one on the street stared, for the Lower East Side was used to citizens wearing their dreams and nightmares. Ice concentrated on the problem. Where could she go? Whom could she go to? Everyone she knew lived here, in the city's underbelly. None of her friends had the clout of the uptown world.

Suddenly, she thought of the Ramseys. She went to the phone and dialed the number they'd given her.

"Yes," Rick's voice answered on the first ring.

"It's Ice."

There was a pause. When Rick spoke, he sounded tense.

"What's wrong?"

Ice told Rick about her sister.

"Can you help out Ice? You asked me to tell you what I know about Baby Sue. I'll do it but first you gotta help me."

"Let me think."

Rick knew Aunt Mandy could probably get Tessa into the Felicia House.

"Look, I think I can help. My aunt runs a halfway house for girls."

"Where it is?"

"At 110th Street."

"That's a lousy neighborhood."

"Don't worry. The place is fully staffed. Since Tessa hasn't broken any law, I'm sure we can get her in there."

"But will it be okay?"

"Sure, Ice. Tessa will be safe there."

15

"It isn't right," Mario said, keeping his voice low so that the staff of the Olliano Pizzeria would not hear him. Sitting opposite Mario, Lieutenant Kushel was biting into Olliano's Saturday Night Special, a pizza with anchovies, sausage, cheese, tomatoes, and onions that Mario had ordered specially for him. Kushel was choking on it.

"Ahhhaabba," Kushel gasped, trying to respond to Mario's direct assault without gagging.

"For Pete's sake. Put the pizza down. Don't they teach you manners in Lithuania?"

"There is no Lithuania," Kushel said, tears in his eyes from his allergic reaction to the onions. Mario misunderstood the source of the water substance. Thinking it sentiment, he grasped the thinner's man blue-veined hand.

"There must have been a Lithuania once," Mario said with great majesty, while gaping at the thin veins visible on Kushel's right hand. "Or there would be no Lithuanians," he continued logically, concentrating on the veins. Then, shrugging his shoulders, he swooped up a large slice of the multi-layered pizza, curled his cherub lips in greeting, and with well-orchestrated aplomb, squashed the whole piece into his mouth, chewing while smiling, his eyes moistening with passion. Then, a second swallow and the hot spicy stuff disappeared entirely before Mario uttered one word because Mario believed people should never speak while eating.

Kushel stared at the man who brought realism and power to everything he did. Kushel knew Mario displayed hot-tempered emotion, yet, in a subtle way, he also conveyed an underlying love of humanity, the personal kind a father would have for a son. This blew Kushel's mind.

"In Italy, things like that happened after the war."

"Like what?" Kushel asked.

"Streets and houses lost their identity. But the Italians wouldn't permit it. In my town, there is a plaque for each house destroyed by the bombs."

Kushel twitched, his fingers trembling as he filled his pipe with Sherlock Holmes' own personal blend, ordered from London through the Sherlock Holmes Mystery Clique Club of which Kushel had been a charter member since he was nine years old.

Mario eyed the uneaten slice of pizza before Kushel.

"Are you sure you're Lithuanian? You don't look Lithuanian," he said nastily.

"What does that mean?"

"You know how it goes in New York. We have looks. The Italian look. The Jewish look. The Irish look. We read people's eyes and their body movements for their identities."

"I am Lithuanian and I do not have an ounce of Italian blood in my veins, thank God," Kushel boasted.

Mario smiled his drop-dead smile, a variation of his drop-dead look, which was more deadly and which members of his community feared.

"How do you know?" he asked, licking his lips for the kill, like a lion going to do battle. "The Romans traveled." He shook his head. "No. You're right. You can't be Italian. If you were, you'd be less judgemental. We are tolerant, after all."

"Tolerant!" Kushel choked on his pipestem. "All I hear from you is how the Italians are the best."

"Well," Mario said brightly, "we are. But that doesn't mean that everybody else isn't equal. We're not fascists, after all."

"Mussolini wasn't a fascist?"

"I named my dog after him." Mario paused in memory of his childhood companion, then added hastily, "Mussolini was a sick man."

Then Mario blew away history with an obsene gesture of his left thumb.

"Now, listen to me, Kushel. I'm like a cop. I know how to talk to criminals on their level. We both know that Rosie and Ricky have been very lucky. My God, they should have been murdered last year. First, by the beasts. Then, by that weirdo."

Kushel nodded in agreement.

"It wasn't the New York City Police Department that saved them. It was me."

"I thought it was a robot."

Mario dismissed history again with another wave of his hand.

"That's how we gotta be. We gotta help out the young. We gotta watch over them or they'll end up bad. Now, listen to me. You gotta close down these clubs on the Lower East Side. My son-in-law tells me that Rosie and he went down there and everybody was very young. Probably eighteen. Imagine! They walk around in garbage wrap. Rick says they trash everything. Even the movies. That's awful."

Like Rick, Mario loved the movies. In fact, the entire SoHo community received their revisionist view of history from the product of the Hollywood golden era. They knew about depression, which many of them had suffered first hand, but Frank Capra told them how noble they were. The women identified with strong ladies like Joan Crawford and Bette Davis as these stars went about the business of trying to make sense of love in the forties' films. Italians were delighted when America imported films with Gina and Sophia because

Hollywood films did not entirely represent their sense of comedy. They simply weren't absurd enough.

To Italians, life is an absurd joke, to be humored as they went on with the business of living so that when the old enemy, death, would come along and sweep them up, they would reside in comfortable houses surrounded by extended families. Italians never feared life. They challenged it to do its worst and best to them while announcing they would survive all catastrophies. Survival was always the main focus of Italian life. In America, this meant to keep separate, keep secrets and keep children pure.

"What was Rosie doing in a place like that?" Kushel nudged at Mario's guilt.

"My daughter is a writer. She's over thirty. She has a husband."

"Yeah . . ."

"It's not her I'm worried about. Rick protects her. And so do you." He smiled. "But this new case . . ."

"Yes, I know."

"That poor girl. She was insulted even in the face of death. Who would remove a dead girl's breasts? Only a maniac."

"But she was a hooker."

"So what. That means her parents failed her," Mario argued. "But she died in honor. She struggled. I understand her body was scarred from this maniac's hand."

"She's still dead."

Mario's steely jade green eyes broke into Kushel's shady grey ones.

"It does not matter when a person dies. It matters how they greet death."

"Mario . . ." Kushel began, "I remember one time a nun was found in the church with her head severed."

"God help us," Mario blessed himself quickly.

"The suspect had thought she was flirting with him and followed her into the church. It was summer and many people were away. When she knelt and said her prayers to God, he put a rope around her neck and strangled her."

"Another maniac," Mario shouted angrily.

"I remembered how he cried. He kept on saying he was sorry. He was sick and two lives were wasted. The nun's and his."

"He should have been crucified," Mario said savagely. "A nun is sacred. Children are sacred. And, we," he pointed to Kushel and himself, "must do our job. We have to close down those clubs. They probably make this kind of life seem glamourous to the kids."

"So do the magazines," Kushel said, frowning.

"Look," Mario said directly. "I'm telling you if you don't do something about that Snake Club, the SoHo community will have to act."

"Like you did with the movie. Baseball bats?" Kushel snarled. "The Mayor doesn't like vigilantes." His lips thinned into a lisp as it always did at the mention of his boss. "So don't get any foolish ideas."

Mario motioned to Kushel with both hands.

"Look, I am an intelligent man. Did we start the violence on West Broadway? No, the cops did. They took out their sticks and we simply defended ourselves. What did you expect us to do? Wait to be hit on the head."

Suddenly, he looked like a Botticelli angel, as he focussed his eyes to the ceiling and blessed himself, his lips smiling, his eyes bright and innocent. Then he looked down at Kushel and snarled again.

"We are not animals. We are simply decent men. If this kind of thing happened in Italy, the clubs would be bombed. The use of young girls for sordid sex? How can men do that? You Americans are sick."

"You mean this never happens in Italy?"

Mario's body suddenly inflated as he moved the pizza to one side of the table, leaned over and grabbed Kushel by his Burberry coat collar.

"We call them animals. They never leave jail alive. Understand?"

Kushel kept calm as he knew his mentor, Holmes, would have, but his teeth were clenching his pipestem and when he trembled, the pipestem spilled over its hot contents on Mario's Pierre Cardin silk shirt.

"*Stupido,*" Mario shouted.

The pizza chef, the waiter and the owner, Olliano, suddenly appeared to see if Mario needed help. The place was empty because Mario had asked them to lock the door so he could have privacy.

"I know that was an accident," Mario said quietly, gesturing his honor guard away.

Kushel reached for his gun, tucked in his pants in the small of his back, a habit he copied from Eddie Murphy in *Beverly Hills Cop*, which his son forced him to see.

"Look, Mario. When I'm angry at other officers, I don't curse at them. First of all, like myself, they carry guns and I can never tell how their wives treated them the night before. Understand me?" he threatened.

Mario didn't flinch but simply stared down the man with great force. Kushel straightened up his back, his shoulders filled out as he concentrated on keeping his dignity under Mario's firebrand concentration. He had learned how to do this during the years he spent on the vice squad watching pimps confront each other without using weapons. They went shoulder to shoulder and would grow taller and taller, until one of them gave in. But this method, used against Mario's *mano a mano* technique, did not work.

Finally, Kushel spoke.

"Mario, I agree with you. Trouble is I've got to get a judge to agree to close down the place. Those clubs have lawyers who can delay legal action. They play for time. For every night they stay open, they earn more loot. You see what I mean?"

"You're not thinking right, as usual," Mario complained.

"You don't go to a judge. You go someplace where the club has no recourse but to obey."

"And where is that?" Kushel asked huffily.

"You go to the fire department."

The Leather Man swung his whip at the teenage girl as the man behind the camera recorded it. Bains, sitting in his private booth, felt hot. In a second, the filming would be finished and the girl would come into the booth to do his bidding. Leather Man heated her up and Bains enjoyed the goodies. The girl would get paid whatever Leather Man had promised and then would be infiltrated into their private ring, to be sent out whenever there was a customer. After a year, she would be shipped to another country for a fresh cycle. By the time she was twenty, she'd be finished, one way or another.

Teenage prostitution and pornography was a lucrative business and Bains was making big bucks on his international roll. He laughed. On Wall Street he'd made his first fortune and now he made billions simply doing what came naturally. And it was illegal, Uncle Sam did not enjoy in the profits.

Under Leather Man's intense whipping, the girl groaned, flecks of rope stunning her body as she screamed, "More."

Bains wet his lips. Good, she did as she was told. He would give her as much as she could take. He signaled the Leather Man to stop and waited for the girl to come to him.

Afterwards, Bains returned to his penthouse. The film operation was installed in a Chelsea warehouse on Ninth Avenue where few passersby would be curious. Upstairs, Bains had created a penthouse for his use whenever he wanted a girl for the night. He had not asked this girl because she was not exciting. Well, he thought, they'll be another.

He jumped into the shower, shampooing his body with Burmese lavender lotion. Showers always made him feel clean. Humming, he put on a robe, and then, accepted the glass of sparkling water his butler held out to him.

"Is there anything else you wish?"

"I'll be leaving for Long Beach within the hour," Bains said.

He tightened the belt on his black terry cloth robe. He was a broad man but his workouts kept his waist very slim. His white hair was tuffed like silk, due to constant supervision, and his steely grey eyes glinted evilly against his skin. His lips were full but whenever he opened his mouth to smile, a slight twitch on the left side caused his face to contort. So Bains did not smile much, preferring to maintain control over everything, especially his nervous system.

His bedroom, too, reflected this need for control. Bains had a preference for black and white, revived with flecks of red. Thus, the entire penthouse had dark interiors, white walls, with touches of red.

In the master bedroom, vertical blinds formed a serpentine backdrop for the dark carpeted platform bed. Opposite the bed was a sitting area boasting a lounge in tufted velvet with leather piping. In a corner, a rococo mirror was suspended behind sprays of ginger flowers in brass bowls from Nepal.

Slowly, Bains walked into the living room. The black leather couches and black velvet carpeting were accessorized with silver candlesticks, mother-of-pearl inlaid boxes, and beautiful red tulips in glazed vases. To the left was a lighter space with a black lacquered grand piano, one of a kind because of the Chinese engravings on its seat. To the right was a long slate table with two Thai jars from 3500 B.C. standing upon it. The walls were upholstered in sound-muffling black flannel and around the table a half-dozen Mies chairs, designed in 1930, stood empty. Next to the table a lacquered bar displayed glasses the color of rose quartz.

On the slate tabletop a spread of canapés awaited his pleasure. Smoked quail with chicory. A flowerlike transparent raw tuna marinated in lime juice, a scattering of dark mushrooms around it. Whitefish with ginger sauce. A neat stack of turnip and crunchy carrot sticks. Scallops in green sauce.

The food awaited his pleasure in front of a tall window

overlooking the Hudson River. Patting his stomach, Bains tasted a few delicacies while watching the night lights of New Jersey. Nighttime eating was bad for the body but he worked it off with sex and jogging.

"The Leather Man wishes to speak to you," the butler announced discreetly.

"Show him in."

The Leather Man looked relaxed though he'd been working hard on the set.

"She wasn't that good. You're losing your touch," Bains complained.

The Leather Man's face stood taut under his mask.

"I have news."

"Well . . ."

"Ice called. She needs big bucks. I think she's ready."

"Have you settled the deal?"

"I need more money to sweeten her up."

He laughed. "Give her anything she wants."

"Alright."

Bains waited for the Leather Man to leave.

"I have a problem."

"What is it?"

"That Caesare dame and her husband are asking questions about . . ."

Bains began to twitch.

"They can't tie us to her."

"There's a twist. It seems that Caesare's husband is Amanda Lord's nephew."

"Shit!"

Leather Man frowned. He knew from past experiences Bains did not like complications.

"What should I do?" he asked.

Bains laughed as he bit into a whitefish canapé.

"I think that Italian cunt deserves a thrill or two. Don't you?" he snarled.

16

"*I have important* information for you. It's about the murder of that poor girl."

The husky voice on the phone was European. Rosie listened to the woman's buttery tones and analyzed that it was the trained voice of a performer, either a singer or an actress.

"What kind of information is it?" Rosie asked quickly, wishing Rick were home instead of doing his daily jogging and chanting stint.

"I can tell you what happened and why it happened."

"How do you know about it?"

"I can't speak over the phone. You'll have to meet me. Please come alone."

"Could you tell me how you got my phone number?"

"Friends."

"But you called me Ms. Caesare."

"I read your book. Everyone knows about you and your husband. You are famous, you know."

"Can you tell me a little more about . . ."

"Do you want this information?" the woman interrupted.

"Yes. Where should we meet?"

"Number Eleven Great Jones Street."

"Apartment number?"

"I'll be in front of the building. But please come alone or I won't show."

"What time?"

"Now."

The woman hung up. Rosie fumed. She'd promised Kushel that she wouldn't do anything on this case without informing him. She'd promised Rick the very same thing. Also, she knew that her father would not like her going out alone to meet an informer.

God, she missed Mario. Their daily phone calls kept her going. Sometimes, they'd talk three or four times a day. Impulsively, she dialed the Casare home. Perhaps Mario would make up today. One never knew.

Celia answered the second ring.

"Hi, Mom. Is Dad home?"

"When are you coming over? You live three blocks away and we never see you. What are you anyway?"

"Mom," Rosie said sweetly. "Could I speak to Dad?"

"You've broken your father's heart. He weeps every day because of your behavior. Why are you making us suffer? Huh? Me, I'm used to it. You never were good to me. You never treated me like a mother. You don't know respect. What time is it?"

"Could you ask Dad to call me, please."

"I gotta go to the bingo game. I'll tell him. But I'm not promising."

Her mother hung up swiftly.

Rosie shrugged. She tried to be nice to Celia but her mother's daily soap operas annoyed Rosie's sense of reality. To Celia, life was never simple. There were always intrigues and traumas, mostly blamed on Rosie's lack of respect. For all his eccentricities, Rosie understood her father well. But she did not understand her mother. Sometimes, she'd worry about this, but then simply would dismiss it. After all, she did love her mother; she simply did not like her views of life.

As many women of her generation, Celia believed that

life was all suffering. This was also common among most Italian women but Rosie's aunts, on the Caesare side of the family, were not like that. Born in Calabria, the world capital for stubborn goddesses, her father's sisters were strong, independent women she'd learned to emulate.

Why her mother was different, Rosie never could fathom. Sometimes she felt her father was responsible. Rosie felt that in an enduring marriage, one person was the star. Her father, being the star type, obviously lived as the star in his marriage, in his fathering of Rosie, and in his life in the SoHo community. If Mario had married a strong, stubborn woman, his marriage would have been a sham.

Then, Rosie's childhood would have been misery instead of simply being ambivalent, like most childrens'.

Her father told her she must be brave and courageous. Her mother hinted she must be silent and smile a lot. Her father told her she could do anything she wanted in this life. Her mother told her to fear everyone, even the grocer. Her father boasted about sex and told her when she was married, she would enjoy it. Her mother told her that she shouldn't be sexy, or she was sure to get raped.

To Rosie, Mario's messages were more exciting. And, if she didn't believe him, she might never have become a writer. And, she would have never fallen in love with Rick.

Rick wasn't Celia's type of man because he was too nice to women. He even washed the dishes, which Celia vowed was a sin against the Madonna. Somehow, Celia thought the Madonna had instructed that women should rule the kitchen and men should rule the bedroom. Rosie hated that way of thinking. To her, things should be mixed up so life would be more exciting.

Since she'd met Rick, he'd been her best friend. He was still her best friend. Before Rick, her father had been her best pal.

Okay, she said to herself. Courage. You wanted to be an investigative reporter. Then you must take chances. This is one of them.

But first, she phoned Kushel's office and left information about her meeting. Then she left the house, leaving a note for Rick.

Broadway was busy with tourists, shoppers, artists, and industrial workers. In its transition to fancy SoHo, the area still had operating factory lofts, though they were definitely on their way out. As Rosie turned down Great Jones Street, she spotted Number 11 and saw it was one of the few industrial loft buildings left in SoHo.

The building was blackened from a century of neglect, an eyesore compared to the newly cleaned facades of the converted loft property. Its large windows were dirty and the fire escapes hadn't been painted for years, though that was against the law.

Rosie walked slowly, taking note that there weren't any people on the street.

Great Jones Street was one of those strange city blocks that led nowhere so that the only pedestrians would be those headed for one of the buildings. But, because it was not a busy street, many large trailer trucks used it for free overnight parking.

When Rosie reached Number 11, she waited outside the doorway. The humming of machines from the industrial lofts upstairs reassured Rosie.

Suddenly, she spotted someone tall, with long blonde braids behind her. Rosie spun about, facing a Wagnerian Viking woman, heavily built, coming at her. The woman grabbed her arms, then she spun Rosie into a web of paralysis, holding her so expertly that Rosie could not move. Systematically, the Viking began beating the young woman until Rosie fell over into a dead faint.

17

"*I'll kill the* son of a bitch who did this to my daughter," Mario screamed as he tore down the hall of St. Mary's Hospital. The nurses and doctors present came to a dead stop at the sight of the burly man running track down their immaculate halls. One aide, wheeling a tray of medicines, swerved to the left. The cart pushed opened a fire exit door and vials of medicine fell down the fire stairs. This caused a minor disturbance because the entire area would have to be fumigated immediately.

Wearing a soft grey Diane Von Furstenberg wraparound and matching sandles and bag, Celia Caesare followed Mario at a safe distance, her hands wrung in despair like the hands of medieval saints always were.

"Mario. Watch yourself. Your heart. Your doctor says you gotta take it easy."

"Animal. Bastard. Wait till I get my hands on you!" Mario announced to all who stood in wonderment at his display of filial devotion.

The two young guards surrounded him.

He stared at them.

"Whaadaya want?"

"May we see your identification?" one asked.

"My daughter is in this place. She's been beaten up by some bastard. Get outa my way!"

"Are you part of a radical group?" a naive guard asked, reaching for his gun.

"Yeah, pretty radical. Fathers who love their daughters," Mario choked on the last word.

"You'll have to come along with us."

He stared at the young men, watching their hands closely.

"If you pull that gun, you're gonna have to use it cause nothing is going to keep me from seeing my Rosa," he stated defiantly.

Aunt Irene, who was tottering behind him on her Joan Crawford black-lizard platform heels, swung her matching black-lizard bag from Florence at one guard's head.

"Hey," he shouted.

The other guard, thinking they were under attack, drew his gun.

"Okay, everybody don't move," he said in terrible English.

"Oh, my goodness. Achoo. Achoo," Aunt Mandy was guarding the rear with Aunt Irene.

"You don't wanna do that," Mario said gently to the guard holding the gun.

"You'll have to come with me to the office," the man said.

Mario smiled at him, temporarily putting him off his guard. Then, with a sudden graceful gesture, like a jackal, Mario swung the boy around, his hand holding the gun so that it fell to the floor, then he bent the man backwards until he screamed: "Don't. Please don't kill me."

A doctor came up to Mario.

"We can't have this kind of thing going on here. We have people dying in this hospital."

"Is this the dying ward?" Mario cried, letting the guard alone. "My baby. My Rosa. Is she dying?"

"Enough," Celia said harshly. "Let's find her room."

"Your wife is right," Aunt Irene added, tugging at her sarong dress that her dressmaker had copied from an old Dorothy Lamour movie.

Mandy watched Irene's movement in shock. First, Irene tugged at the hipline of the dress that was much too tight.

Because she'd been sitting for so long in her limo during the long ride from Southhampton, though the car was air-conditioned, her form-fitting dress clung precariously to her chubby buttocks. Everyone could see that Aunt Irene was a free woman who simply did not believe in girdles, for the outline of her fancy Parisian bikinis were obvious.

Because she was nervous, Aunt Irene checked the inside of her low V-neck dress to be certain that her huge breasts were firmly encased in her specially built brassiere. This structure, also from Paris, was designed in lace and silk and had stiff bones pleated into it so that Irene's breasts never sagged. It also narrowed Irene's waist so that she looked much slimmer, but as a result, the remainder of her soft flesh outpoured at the hips and gave her an hourglass figure, popular in her parents' time, but not now.

Mandy watched Irene check her breasts and turned away in horror. Irene smiled, pushing her lips together to smooth her shocking purple lipstick with her tongue. She smiled again, not realizing that the lipstick had smeared all over her teeth. Mandy shuddered.

"Mario, take it easy," Irene put her hand on her brother-in-law's shoulder.

"You're right. I must remain calm," he agreed.

His eyes were at half-mast, limpid, sad, teary.

"She's gonna be alright," Irene said. "Our Rosie is strong. Where is Rick, by the way?"

"He's probably in the room with her, where we should be," Mandy snickered, tired of the Italians' melodrama. "Achoo, Achoo," she sneezed on schedule.

Dressed in a Bill Blass coatdress of powder-blue pinstripe, Mandy wore a long string of white pearls, matching white gloves and white spectator pumps. Under her white straw safari hat, her hair was smooth. Her ears were dotted with tiny diamond earrings and on her ring finger she wore a diamond wedding band. In the midst of her nephew's Italian in-laws, Mandy seemed out of place.

She examined them. Celia looked calm and well dressed but Irene looked like a chorus girl after a performance in 1939. Mario's silk suit was wrinkled from his insistent anxiety. No, Mandy thought logically, none of these people understand how to display grace under pressure.

"Achoo, Achoo," she sneezed again. "Oh, Sonny," she complained between sneezes, "I wish you were here."

"Maybe he's running," Celia suggested. "If he was out on one of his runs, the cops probably haven't reached him yet. You know how fast Ricky runs."

"Those cops took a long time getting to us," Irene added. "It's a good thing I was having lunch with Mario or I might not be here."

"Lieutenant Kushel called me personally," Mandy boasted to all. "He told me that Rosie was hurt."

Irene gave her a dirty look as two nuns, dressed in white, came up to the group. They were Sisters of Charity and their headresses looked like a pioneer woman's hat. One nun was very thin; the other was very plump. Both had rosy cheeks and sparkling eyes.

"We know you're upset, sir," they said to Mario, "but you must listen to the doctors."

"Where are the doctors?" he demanded.

"They're very busy," the nuns replied, defending the producers of multimillion dollar incomes.

"Those doctors don't have no compassion anymore," Irene flipped her pinky at the nuns.

On her finger an eight-carat diamond startled the religious duo. Spotting it, both bowed their heads in prayer.

"Where is Mrs. Ramsey?" Mandy asked, yearning to introduce clarity into this Italian drama.

"Room six-twelve. But you can't visit unless you're immediate family," a nurse said from the desk.

The nurses had been watching this dramatic interruption with interest.

"We are all immediate family," Celia announced. Then she took the lead. "Come on. Let's go."

Mario hurried after her. Irene toddled quickly, outflanking Mandy's somber walking pumps. The guards followed, but the nuns reassured them that this was simply an Italian family who cared and not a radical fringe group ready to bomb the hospital because of its anti-Third World attitudes. Besides, Italians never bombed, the nuns whispered. The guards agreed, knowing Italians specialized in murder.

The door to Room 612 was opened. On the bed, wrapped in bandages, was Rosie. Her emerald green eyes were the only spots of recognition. The rest of Rosie, where she wasn't bandaged, was the color of purple. At her bedside, Rick, in jogging shorts and a sweaty T-shirt, was on his knees, chanting.

"Rosa," Mario ran to her side.

The private nurse was startled. Jumping up, she put a finger to her lips.

"Shhhh. She's resting."

"My Rosa. My darling. Forgive me," Mario sobbed, getting down on his knees beside Rick. "Ricky, how could you let me not speak to my daughter?"

Rick bowed his head guiltily. Then, in a row behind him, Irene and Celia knelt and began to recite their Catholic prayers. Mandy, keeping her Protestant distance, refused to kneel before the cross of Christ, hung in regal evidence above Rosie's bed.

Mario spotted rosary beads at the side of the bed.

"My God, is she dying?" he screamed, knowing that rosaries were a ritual in terminal illness.

"She's coming along fine," the nurse insisted. "Does her doctor know you're here?"

"Who's her doctor? I'm her father."

Standing up quickly, Celia took the nurse aside, explaining that Mario was the dramatic type and Rosie was his only daughter so that the nurse should be patient. Irene stood up and reached into her lizard bag. Then she gave the nurse a one-hundred-dollar bill and told her to shut up. Mandy handed the nurse flowers she'd bought at a florist.

"Would you put these in a vase for dear Rosie, please," she said calmly. "Achoo, Achoo."

"Rose fever?" the nurse queried.

"Rosie fever," Celia admonished.

Surrounding the bed, they waited for their beloved girl to speak. Though her eyes seemed half-opened, Rosie was distant, dreaming in the universe of Demerol.

Rick, more emotional than the family had ever seen him, remained on his knees, whispering chants.

"Nam Myho Renge Kyo. Nam Myho Renge Kyo."

"Is he crazy? Why is he reciting Chinese?" Mario demanded.

Mandy shook her head slowly.

"Sonny is simply—achoo—meditating."

"Do you still have that cold? Stay away from Rosa," Mario warned. Then added, "You've had a cold ever since I know you."

"It's not a cold, it's an allergy," Mandy explained, dabbing her nose with her fine linen handkerchief.

She walked over to the far side of the room near the window, hoping that the cool air from the air-conditioning unit would filter out her allergic feelings about Italians. Looking down at the narrow Village street below, she watched pedestrians scurry back and forth, to work, to home, to play, unaware that in this large grey building, life and death commanded. Stoically, Mandy wiped a tear from her eyes. Whenever she was in a hospital, Mandy thought of Eric, her late husband, and of all the time she'd spent waiting for him to die peacefully. Eric in New York. Felicia in Italy. She hadn't been with Felicia at the end, but the authorities told her death occurred quickly.

"How is the food here?" Celia asked when the nurse returned with the vase of roses.

"She can't eat yet. Her jaw is bruised."

"Broken? Or bruised?" Mario demanded.

"Bruised."

"*Nam Myho Renge Kyo.*"

"Rick, will you get up from that Chinese meditation or whatever the hell it is, and talk to me. What's wrong with her? Is she seriously hurt? Will anything be permanent? Talk."

Rick looked up, his face in anguish. Seeing his son-in-law's despair, Mario put his arm around the younger man's shoulders.

"Come on, fella. Let's get up and walk around a bit."

"I'm not going to leave her. I should never have left her. Why wasn't I with her?" Rick murmured.

"What actually happened?"

"We don't know for sure. She called Kushel and said she was running down a phone tip. He wasn't there so she left a message. I should have been home. When she gets better, I'll never leave her alone again. Never!"

"Rosie wouldn't like that, Rick," Mario warned. "You know how independent our girl is."

"You can't blame yourself, Sonny," Mandy said.

"So who can he blame?" Irene asked, sitting on the room's only armchair, her legs crossed so Mandy could see her lace bikinis.

At the sight of Irene's underwear, Mandy began twitching.

"What's wrong, Amanda?" Irene asked. "Are you getting worse?"

"It seems so," Mandy answered. "Sonny, Rosie will be alright, won't she?"

"The doctors say she'll be okay in a week or so," the nurse added. "She's got to heal. You know how bruises are. It's like a fighter in a ring," she said to Mario, searching for a metaphor he would understand.

"Yeah, she's a fighter," he announced to one and all. "My Rosie is a champion." He pounded his chest proudly. "A real champ."

Hearing Mario's pronouncement of her bravery and courage, Rosie's eyes flew open. She focussed on the faces of her loved ones. Then she forced her bruised lips opened.

"Daddy?" she moaned.

Mario took Rosie's hand and pressed it to his lips. Kissing it tenderly, he wiped her forehead gently with his other hand. Then he leaned over and whispered, "How do you feel, my darling? Your daddy is here," Mario said softly. "You're safe."

Standing behind Mario, Rick's body slackened. Slowly he walked outside the room. In the hall, he seemed lost for a moment. Then, tears filled his eyes. Hiding in an alcove, Rick wiped them away hastily.

18

"Yeah, Mario, I closed down the club but it's opened again. I told you it's next to impossible to keep those sleazy joints shut down," Kushel said on the phone in a harried tone.

"Didn't you go to the fire department?"

"Naw. The chief was away in Bermuda and his deputy refused to take action. We have to wait a week."

"Meanwhile, more kids could be harmed. We gotta have action now."

"Sorry, Mario. Cannot do."

"What about the woman?"

"Well, Rosie's description is vague but I put it on the wire. I wish she'd seen more of her."

"What is this world coming to, when women beat up women? I guess weirdos are weirdos, whatever sex they are."

"Mario," Kushel said, "I hope you're not going to do anything foolish."

"What do you mean?"

"I hope you're not going to send your baseball bats out."

"Hey, Lieutenant, what are you talking about?"

"You know what I'm talking about."

"This conversation has come to an end," Mario said hastily. "Good-bye."

He turned his attention to his appearance.

"Hey, Celia. Help me dress," he called to his wife.

Celia was brewing minestrone for Rosie's lunch. She'd already decided that the food at St. Mary's would kill her daughter and was personally going to do something about this.

She walked into the bedroom.

"Mario, what do you think you're doing?"

His eyes were all innocence.

"Help me dress, Celia. I'm late."

She wiped her hands on her apron. Underneath, she wore a softly printed blue and white dress, which was tightly belted around her slim waistline. White pearls around her neck and white and blue spectator pumps completed her Fifth Avenue matron look. Celia was dressed for the hospital. After checking the dietitian's chart and realizing that only bland American food in small portions would be served to her healing daughter, Celia decided she would cook a nutritious lunch each day and serve it to Rosie herself.

She loved Rosie, but somehow they couldn't get along. Celia didn't understand why this was so. She'd been brought up in a small Italian town where the mark of love was criticism. No one ever said, "I love you." What they said, was, "watch out you're getting fat" or "keep quiet, you talk too much." In an Italian family, that meant, "I love you."

Women complained and fretted and to their children this was supposed to be interpreted as signs of love. Only during courtship did women keep their mouths shut. If they insulted their suitor, they'd never marry and then life would be a sham. There was nothing as scandalous as an unmarried woman in a small Italian town. However virtuous, she was the target of constant gossip. Clever women married young and then went about the business of living. Isn't that what their own Sophia Loren had done? Yes, Celia nodded. Sophia was a very smart lady. She was married. Had sons. Had a career.

When Rosie was growing up, and showing signs of being

totally independent of these values, Celia worried. When Rosie met Rick, Celia was frightened. Not only was he terribly good looking but he was wealthy. To Celia's peasant soul, this meant the marriage could not last. Besides, he was American and everyone knew they believed in divorce.

She watched her beloved husband teach Rosie all the values that he would have taught a son. Celia felt guilty because she'd given him only one child. But she was frightened for her daughter. It was alright to teach sons to be independent, but a daughter? Never! A woman had to learn her place. She had to learn not to challenge men, or society, then she could have everything she wanted.

But her daughter did not turn out this way. She challenged everything. When Rosie decided to live in sin with Rick, Celia had a quiet breakdown. She walked around SoHo with her head bowed in shame, though it was 1969 and all rules had changed in America. But to Italians, these rules were the same. Good women were wives and virgins. Everyone else was a whore.

Two years later, when Rick married Sharon Neiman, Celia had to bite her tongue not to say to her daughter, you see, our rules are right. He's had you and now he's after someone else. Since her daughter's heart was broken, Celia said nothing. She only glared and that sent enough negative messages, so Rosie never came to Celia for solace or support. Rosie always went to Mario for that.

Celia knew when all this started. Since birth, Mario treated his daughter like a princess. He checked everything. Her crib. Her bottle. Her diapers. Her food. Often he scolded Celia for not taking care of their princess in a royal way. Celia did not fight. But she resented this extravagant attention to her daughter. After all, she was only a daughter, not a son.

But she gave Mario no sons and had to live with this sadness. Then, sadness turned into bitterness at Rosie's eccentric behavior. And the chasm between them grew.

When Rick came back to Rosie and they decided to get married, Celia told her daughter to reject him. Rosie said no, she loved Rick. To Celia's surprise they seemed happy. For a while she was content, but then her daughter began writing those awful books.

Confused about her relationship with Rosie, Celia always did her duty. She cooked the best foods. She would give anything to Rosie, if her daughter asked. But Rosie never did. So Celia devoted her life to being good. In the night, she prayed that Rosie would get pregnant and have a child so she could start all over again. She would be more successful with a grandchild. But Rosie and Rick decided not to have a family. Why, she did not know. For Celia, children were the real jewels of life.

"Stop fidgeting," Mario shook Celia from her thoughts. "Get my shirt."

Mario stood in the center of their bedroom, waiting for Celia to lay his outfit on the bed. Then, slowly, he dressed, his wife helping him. Finally, he smoothed down the lapels of his Giorgio Armani gray silk suit and was ready to begin his day.

"Mario, where are you going?"

"You do your job and I'll do mine. You're taking the minestrone to Rosie?"

She nodded.

"But, Mario," she touched the upsweep coiffeur which Aunt Irene insisted she get in the face of the new emergency. Aunt Irene always believed in greeting life's grim realities with a new beauty treatment and hairdo.

"Don't worry about me, Celia," he swept her into his arms and kissed her hard on the mouth. He'd always kissed her that way, as sweethearts, and as man and wife.

She melted and put her head on his shoulder.

"Don't cry," he said hoarsely. "I'm going to do some business. That is all."

She looked up at him with misty dark eyes.

"But where?" she insisted.

"I'll be at the club. Have a good day and tell Rosie I'll drop by later this afternoon," he said.

Watching him leave, Celia began to pray. She liked to chat directly with God. "Watch out for Mario," she prayed.

As Mario strolled down Prince Street toward the club, he waved to many passersby, all of whom asked for Rosie.

"She's getting better."

"Her mother is bringing her minestrone."

"Her husband is praying in church."

These replies satisfied his neighbors' curiosity. They were all well-wishers in the face of trauma. Yet they loved to gossip about Rosie, her marriage to that American, and her strange hobby of finding bodies and writing about them. The Italians simply didn't understand but they knew she had plenty of money, which earned their respect. Also, she was Mario's daughter, which meant she was royalty.

Mario entered the private men's club silently, but Crazy Nuz greeted him with a three-decker hero sandwich with his favorite fillings, three kinds of salami.

"You hungry, Mario?" Nuz asked.

"Something light."

"Half of this?"

"A quarter."

Nuz shook his head in disapproval. Then he went back to the counter, took a huge bread knife, sliced the sandwich in half, then in quarters.

Mario sat at an empty table. He wasn't hungry but knew it was an insult to refuse Nuz's food.

Nuz served him the sandwich.

"Espresso?"

"Yeah. Are the guys around?"

"Yeah, they're here. See."

He pointed to the door where Lefty, Willie the Worm, and Montana Tommy walked in. Dressed in jogging suits, they did not look Italian at first glance. When they sat at Mario's table and kissed both his cheeks as greeting, their true nature was revealed.

"What are we going to do?" Lefty asked.

"Baseball bats?" Montana Tommy suggested mysteriously.

Slowly, Mario bit into the salami sandwich. Chewing each morsel slowly, he relished the spicy taste. They waited quietly, knowing Mario's strict edict about not talking while eating. Finally, he finished the snack and sipped the espresso. Then, wiping his mouth with a napkin, he gestured to the men to lean closer.

"These Lower East Side people wear chains and things. I don't think baseball bats will work against them."

"Guns?" Crazy Nuz suggested.

"You know the cops don't like guns," Willie the Worm said.

"Yeah, they go crazy," Lefty agreed.

"They'll be no cops around, don't worry. But we don't carry guns because we are not beasts. We are decent law-abiding citizens. Right?" Mario said.

"Right," they agreed.

"Okay, I got a pal at the police station who's going to block any calls," Mario explained.

"So what'll it be?" Nuz asked.

"We don't want to hurt anyone. We simply want to scare them. Right?" Mario asked.

"Right," they said.

"The *boys* would take care of them if asked," Lefty observed.

"We're not going to do something stupid like that," Mario said. "Remember. Whenever you ask those guys for something, you owe them your life."

They all nodded. The group had known each other since childhood on the streets of SoHo. They were working men and had never done anything illegal. But, they had always protected their homes and families.

"We gotta think of something scary," Willie the Worm said.

"I got it," Nuz jumped up.

"What?"

"Tear gas. The SWAT teams always use it on television."

"Those dopers would love it," Mario observed.

"Well, how about that stuff they use on dogs?"

"That's it," Mario jumped up.

"What?"

"Dogs. We'll go out to Angelo Nuceo. He trains those greyhounds for the beasts. You know, the ones that guard their mansions. Angelo says those dogs can do anything."

"Dogs?" the group frowned.

"Yeah, he's got real big ones," Mario stated.

The Snake Club was getting ready for its night games. At midnight, the bar was filled with regulars in the usual leather, plastic, and other strange garb. A Mick Jagger video was playing in the back room and people were watching it, some standing, some dancing. At the bar, Fat Man was smoking a cigar. The bartender, a coke dealer, was coughing from the cigar's fumes.

"Don't you like tobacco?" Fat Man asked.

"I'm allergic to it."

"Here's some more."

Fat Man blew smoke into the man's face. It turned him red with fury. But he needed this job. He coughed up saliva into the wastebasket and filled his orders. Coca-Cola. Pepsi. Rum and Ginger. Sweet Wine. And cocaine. Regulars were streaming into the bar and copping coke, then running into the john to taste their purchase. Fat Man watched, knowing that all the action put more money into his bank account.

A sadomasochistic crowd was sitting at a table in one corner. A tall blond man dominated the conversation. He was the local king at the Snake Club. This regal spot changed hands often, given to whoever supplied the best dope. Someone would suddenly come into the area and have a new supply and generate excitement into this bored crowd. This latest king was the son of a German count who rode around in a long blue limo with flocks of girls. Now, the girls fussed over him, sitting on his lap, getting drinks, spoiling him dreadfully.

Fat Man laughed at this spectacle. He'd seen these dope kings come and go, thinking they had it made. But no one controlled this scene except the Fat Man.

Two huge black belts were standing about the bar, keeping order. It was a damp night. The day had been drizzly gray. It was more annoying than an actual downpour because one never knew whether it was wet or not. Fat Man had gone to the bank several times. Each time, mid-route, it had started to drizzle. Sweating, he ordered another cognac, hoping he wouldn't get more sweats tonight.

The door opened. Fat Man came to attention. Two well-dressed men walked into the Club. Were they businessmen or cops? He wasn't sure. He signalled security to keep them covered.

"What can I do for you?"

"We'd like to have a talk with you."

"What about?"

"We're neighbors."

"I've never seen you around here."

"We're from the West. SoHo."

"Looking for thrills?"

"We're not your type," Lefty explained. "We need to talk to you about something important."

Fat Man realized the men were Italian and leaped to the assumption that they were Mafia.

"Hey, I pay Fat Angelo plenty."

"We're not beasts," Lefty shouted. "We're fathers. We have daughters. Look at these kids." He pointed to the young people at the bar who were watching this scene with passive amusement, their standard reaction to life.

"They're adults," Fat Man was getting impatient with these gooks. He waved for his bodyguards. Suddenly, three men, dressed in jogging suits, entered. Each held onto three large greyhounds. The regulars, aware that something different was happening, began to scatter. Most reached the exit quickly.

Fat Man watched his disloyal patrons leave him in the lurch.

"What do you guys want?" he said, watching his black belts cower in face of the dogs.

"We told you, it's better that this club be closed down, right away," Willie the Worm stated.

"No way."

"I see."

Montana Tommy gestured.

The men came forward. In the back room, the video was screaming obscene lyrics which caused them to shake their heads in disbelief.

"So, what's your final answer?" Lefty asked.

"Fuck you," Fat Man said.

"You shouldn't use vulgar words like that," Lefty said. "But I'm a patient man. I'll let you leave your club."

Fat Man walked out of the club quickly. In a corner phone booth, he called the police station and was assured that the police were on their way.

Inside the club, the three men unleashed the dogs. The greyhounds enjoyed their work. They bit into every table, every chair, every wood partition. After twenty minutes, the place looked as if it had been bombed.

The three men blew a whistle and the dogs came to strict attention.

"Okay, it's time to go," Lefty said, viewing the wreckage.

Outside, Fat Man waited.

"You'll pay for this," he swore.

"No, *you* will," Lefty pointed his finger at Fat Man's face. "If you open this club again. You're getting off easy. We don't believe in killing people, even animals like you who destroy children."

Then Lefty and his friends, dogs in tow, got into three unmarked vans and disappeared.

19

"*I've been sitting* around all day, staring at the ceiling. I was hungry but too lazy to get up and eat. All I felt was an emptiness. So I forced myself to clean up, did my hair and went out to eat on Second Avenue. I said to myself, Ice, your life is ruined. Without the Snake Club you're nothing. That's when I decided I had to do the porno movie. Do you understand, Mr. Ramsey?"

Rick looked at the beautiful girl who should have been treated as a princess. She reminded him of Rosie, though they did not look alike. Yet, Ice had Rosie's fierce determination to defeat life, though to Ice, life was sordid, unlike Rosie's views.

"Ice, try to call me Rick, won't you?" he suggested gently.

She nodded her ice blue hair.

"Look, honey, once you take that step, there's no escape." Rick was trying not to sound like a Lutheran pastor, but he was feeling like one. All of his Protestant Connecticut guilt was heaped upon him because he had failed. His beautiful wife lay bruised in the hospital. Because of painkillers, she'd been conscious only a few minutes in the past few days. Yet, each time she opened her eyes she called for Mario, not Rick.

Rick tried to understand. He knew Rosie and her father had a strange, close bond, almost unshakable, even in the face of adversity. But he'd thought that he would be first in her heart after they became man and wife. Rosie said he was her best friend, her lover, her husband, yet, lying there, in the dark recesses of her pain, she called for her father. Rick felt he had not earned a strong place in the dark psyche of her inner being, or she would call for him.

In the last few days, Rick had moped about the loft, refusing calls from the Caesare family, even those in California who'd heard about Rosie's plight. Arnoldo, sensing Rick's pain, had offered to buy dinner. Arnoldo was a cheapo type so Rick knew he must look terrible if Arnoldo was springing. But Rick said no, thanks, another time, to the electronic S and M nut.

Nothing helped. Rick lay on their bed, thinking of Rosie. He walked into her closet and touched her favorite clothes. He sat at the white grand paino, remembering the moments of happiness there, when Rosie always smiled. Then he thought about what life would be without her and knew he could not go on alone.

There was no danger that Rosie would die. The doctors said that she was merely bruised but they were concerned about the bruises on her rib cage. Then, they announced nothing was broken. She would be back among the living as soon as the shock wore off. But the shock of seeing his adorable, strong, energetic Rosie, in a bed, lying there without her normal energy terrified Rick, so he chanted. He prayed that he would die first. Rosie could survive his death but he couldn't survive hers.

Still, his ego was deeply hurt. The pain of her not asking for him was greater than it should be. He chanted and tried to squelch ego needs, but he still felt bad. He should think of Rosie, and not himself. But he came to the conclusion that he was still suffering from that disease known as male chauvinism. Though Rosie and he had worked on changing this, it was still strong. Rosie always said that one of the first things she'd liked about Rick was that he was tall and attractive and didn't seem to know it. Rosie was gorgeous and didn't seem to know it either. People said they were a beautiful couple. The magazines were writing about them as the "In" Couple, the Very Modern Couple. Whenever they saw this media hype, they laughed. While hype sold books and earned royalties, they simply wanted to be in love and be happy.

Since they were writers, they worked very hard. Rosie had a theory that when a person was disciplined in her personal life, a person was also disciplined in her profession. Because of Rosie's edicts, borrowed from the Romans, Rick and she were very disciplined. Mario had done a good job. He'd groomed his daughter to look at life with all its harshness and then go out and score.

Rosie scored. That's why Ice reminded him of his wife. Ice had that same kind of courage. Sitting opposite her, Rick examined Ice's soft body, remembering how she'd looked while performing partly nude. While Rosie was a Renoir, Ice was a Mondrian. Rosie was blessed with a soft Mediterranean aura while Ice's beauty was diluted into a fine slim line of ascetic harshness.

"Ice," Rick asked. "What about the Snake Club attracts you so?"

Her dark eyes glistened as she spoke, watching him warily.

"I created somebody beautiful there, someone who was satanically dark with the black clothes and the smell of leather. I was out there in the universe and didn't care what else was going on because all those dudes came to the Club to pay me for anything I wanted to trash. I felt out of this world. A fantasy. I was the best dresser around. The best dancer around. I could get any guy who walked in there. I was Ice, with my jet black stockings. I was my own personal video. All by myself, I created excitement. All the unwanted ones came to the club to adore me. I was the princess of the underworld. I was Ice Goddess."

She paused, licking her lips, their natural strawberry color made her look younger than her seventeen years.

"And it's all gone. The Snake Club is closed. I got no money. And I need bucks to get Tessa out of that halfway house and set up a pad for us. I need big bucks to get her into a good school. I got to produce."

Rick felt an immediate rush of warmth for the girl who looked vulnerable and needy, her beauty glowing through her pain.

Ice noticed. She began staring at him, her eyes were deep pools of seductive darkness.

"Ice, I can give you money for Tessa."

"No way. I don't take money from strangers."

"I'm not a stranger."

"Yes, yes, you are."

"You called me when you needed help. Twice."

"I had nobody else."

"It's more than that."

She touched Rick's hand and he suddenly felt hot.

"Yes, Rick, there's much more than that."

Rick was stunned by Ice's experienced sexual play. Then he realized he was becoming mesmerized by her and drew away. The first time he'd lost his head he'd married Sharon Neiman who had turned his life completely around. Rick had never really understood why. He didn't really like Sharon. She was tall, and looked like a giraffe with the same type of above-it-all look. She was rich and knew the scenes around the globe. Rick had followed Sharon from party to party. Then, one day, he had come to his senses and wondered where his beloved Rosie was.

Whenever he thought about his mistake, he'd come to the conclusion he'd suffered from a temporary mental illness, like the bug soldiers caught in the Far East which caused malaria. When they were cured, the disease could be revived quickly. So, Rick thought, my disease is being revived, but this time I'm not giving into it.

Rick looked at Ice sitting on the chair like a baby rabbit who wanted to be cuddled. Suddenly, Ice jumped up and settled into his lap. Rick felt hot again. They were sitting in an empty SoHo restaurant in the middle of the afternoon, too late for lunch and too early for cocktails. Several waitresses looked at Rick and shook their heads warily. They were mourning his oncoming death if Rosie ever found out.

Ice put her arms around Rick's neck and pressed her soft lips to his. He felt like mush. But he remembered, Ice was a child and he was married to Rosie. Gently, he pushed her away.

"Ice, please sit in your chair. I want to say something to you."

"You're a cute daddy," she sangsong, flirting with him.

"Ice, I'm not your daddy. I'm Rick Ramsey and I'm married to Rosie Caesare. Remember that."

"She's nasty."

"No, she's not. You two got started on the wrong track. You're a lot alike. Now, I want to say this to you. Ice, you're a beautiful, wonderful girl and you're going to grow up to be a beautiful, wonderful woman. But I'm madly in love with my wife. Do you understand?"

She laughed at Rick, disbelieving.

"No dude has ever said no to Ice," she said proudly.

Rick held her hand affectionately, not wanting to bruise her fragile ego.

"I'm not saying no. I'm saying that if I were your age and I were single, I would be after you. But that's not the way it is."

"You want me. You're hot. I can see it."

"Yes, that's true."

"Then why don't we fuck."

He flinched, his erection was growing, disloyal to Rosie in her hospital bed.

"No, we're not going to do that."

"Why not? Are you some kind of sadist creep?"

"I hope not. I'm an ordinary husband in love."

"You mean you don't screw around," she said, trashing all.

"Ice, let me tell you a secret. I was unfaithful to Rosie one sad time and almost lost her. I vowed that I would never do it again. Do you understand, Ice? Do you understand that there are things that are more important than an orgasm?"

"Like what?"

"Like love, for instance."

"Don't know anything about love," she sangsong.

"Yes, you certainly do."

She shook her head stubbornly.

"Sure you do," he insisted. "You've been telling me you have to take care of Tessa. That's love."

"My sis is not a dude. I never loved a dude."

"You will."

"No, I never will." She took a deep breath. "I've had many dudes in heat, but that's not love. I used to dream sometime of having someone to love me always, to wake me up in the morning with that tornado, and put me to sleep in the night. Sure, I dream about love. But people only talk about it. Nobody loves."

"Some try."

"I do. I try. But is that love? I mean, I try to be around if I'm needed. Look, I don't go walking around telling some dude every four minutes that I love him. But if someone's a friend, and needs me, I'll be there. Look, sometimes kids get sad. I know what that's like. So I say to my buddies, call me and we'll hang out. I was always alone. My mother hated me. What was I supposed to do? Was I supposed to kiss her feet while she was doing me no good?" She gasped again. "Look, I thought I'd meet a superman who would be all fire and sweep me away from all of this. But I never met him because dudes only want to fuck me. They don't want to love me."

Her face turned pink with the onset of panic.

"I'm on the verge of losing my mind, Rick. I have to hold onto my mind or there goes Ice."

"You'll be okay."

"I used to be hungry for life but I'm tired of this agony," she sangsong the words. "I'm yellow inside. Undernourished. Nothing makes sense to me anymore. But then, I sing and I control my life, especially for the crowd. I have to be Ice Goddess." She turned toward him again. "Does this make any sense to you?"

"Yes, I understand how you feel."

"Since I was fifteen, I ran around with that pack on the Lower East Side. It worked for a while. We were sinister. We were a family. The unwanted ones. Our mothers and fathers had hurt us bad. We all hated them. So we made up our own family of the unwanted and the dummies. We would talk only to ourselves, mix only with ourselves, even when we hated each other. We were the beautiful demons in leather and spikes. We were a pack of black, wild things on the street and everyone got out of our way. But then, it all got crazy. People began dying." She stopped and looked at him seriously. "There were gang fights. Guys kicked other guys in the head. It was Clockwork Orange time. And then came the disease. Now it's virus time."

She paused, folding her hands quietly, her shiny purple nails glinting in the daylight.

"I wanted a way out. I didn't know what. For a while I did drugs, but then my mind started to explode. When I started singing, I got relief from my pain. Fat Man asked me to sing at the Club. Since then, everything's been okay. You know what I mean. I'm cooled out."

Rick picked up her hands, brought them to his lips, kissed them gallantly.

"That's a kiss for a lady," she pouted. "I'm no lady."

"You will be."

"Naw, I'm about to run around in the buff in front of the camera. Some lady."

"Take my money, Ice. Let me help you."

"No," she said stubbornly. "I'm too proud."

"But we'll say it's a loan."

"No, thank you."

Rick wondered what he could do to save her from the porno business.

"Rick. Are you really serious?" she began singsonging again. "You really don't want to fuck me?"

"It wouldn't be good, Ice. Not for me. And not for you. You see that, don't you?"

She shook her head, too sad for her young years. Her head bowed, she whispered in a strange voice, "Does your wife know how lucky she is? You're a good dude."

"I'm the lucky one. Rosie gives me everything she's got, all the time. Now how many men have a woman like that?"

Ice was quiet.

"I heard she got beat up bad," she finally said.

"She's okay. Ice, do you know anything about a tall woman with long blonde braids?"

She thought about it.

"Uh, uh. We've had some crazies but not one with braids."

"Rosie didn't get a good look at her."

"I'll ask around."

"I'd appreciate that. Look, call me whenever you want to talk. Okay?"

Her eyes got shiny.

"Rick, you're a buddy," she said.

"I'd like to be your buddy, Ice."

"I still think we'd have a great fuck."

"Sure we would," he agreed. "But you're going to find someone else out there."

"Don't know," she sangsong as she got up from the chair. "Daddy wouldn't like it."

Then she walked out of the restaurant, holding her head high.

Rick jogged to St. Mary's. On the way, he thought about how stupid he'd been in the last few days. What was wrong with Rosie's asking for her dad? She was probably feeling like a little girl because of her bruises.

When he reached the hospital, Rick ran up the stairs to Rosie's room. The private nurse smiled at him.

"She's been awake several times today," she reported.

"Was anyone here?"

"Her mother brought lentil soup. Her father brought those roses."

The nurse pointed to a table filled with dozens of red roses, Rosie's favorite flower.

"And both aunts came," the nurse added.

"She has many more."

"Some family." She smiled. "She's due to wake up soon."

"Is she feeling better?"

"Yes, and she's been calling for you, Mr. Ramsey."

"Really."

He sat at the side of the bed, watching Rosie's lovely face.

"I'm going to be here for a while. Why don't you take a break," he suggested to the nurse.

"That's nice of you."

Rick concentrated on Rosie. She looked like a painting in sleep, too beautiful to be real. Then, her lips moved. Her eyes fluttered. When she saw Rick, she smiled.

"Ricky, darling," she whispered.

Rick kissed her lips, her cheeks, her hair.

"I love you, Rosie," he whispered.

"Love you, too," she murmured weakly.

Rick buried his face in the crook of Rosie's neck, feeling her fragile warmth. Then, his face against her, he wept.

20

A *week had past* since Rosie's unfortunate "incident," as she had begun to call it. Her energy had returned and she was anxious to leave the hospital. She felt very much loved. Each day, her mother brought her a specially cooked lunch. For the first time in years, they were able to have small conversations without fighting. Rosie realized that when no one else was around, they got along okay.

Each afternoon, after Celia left, Mario arrived to check out the hospital. The nurses and doctors, used to his demands about his daughter's comfort, greeted him warily when he appeared, list in hand.

"Her room is too hot."

"Her bed is too high."

"Her color has not improved."

"There's too much noise from the street."

The staff tried to do what it could to fill Mario's wishes, knowing that in a day or two, Rosie would be leaving. She was fortunate, for none of her bruises were permanent. Detective Kushel told Mario that Rosie was attacked by a real pro who only wanted to frighten her, not to maim her permanently.

Mario and Kushel conferred on who this pro was. Mario

had sent word out onto the SoHo streets about the Viking woman but no one reported seeing anyone like her. Besides, women were rarely used for this kind of work.

"Huh, Women's Lib. First the weirdo. Now the Viking," Mario complained to Kushel.

"It's true. Women don't usually do stuff like this. There only have been one or two."

"Yeah and both of them were after my Rosie," Mario swore. "They don't know Rosie won't scare easily."

He was right. Rosie was not frightened. She was eager to return to the project. When Rick arrived, usually at dinnertime, all Rosie would talk about was when she could leave the hospital.

"Soon," he said.

They had invented a system for privacy. First, they'd tell the nurse to take a long dinner hour. After the solemn nurse would go to dinner, Rosie would eat supper. When the aide would take the tray away, Rick would sneak into bed.

"It's like Hemingway," she said.

"*A Farewell to Arms*," he agreed.

There were a few times when Rick and Rosie had made love though they did not want to cause a scandal mainly because Mario would be furious and tell them sex was a private affair and not supposed to take place in a hospital room.

After they made love, Rick told Rosie about Ice.

"She's set to do a porno movie because the Club was closed down."

"What happened?"

"It was attacked by dogs."

"Dogs?"

"Yeah, but I think a certain person who shall be nameless was behind it all. At least, that's what Kush thinks."

"Kushel is always wrong."

"I don't know. This time he could be right."

She stared at him, her eyes not betraying the fact that she knew he was talking about Mario.

"You like that girl, don't you Rick?" she said finally.

"She's a kid who's never had anyone be nice to her," he said seriously. "Can't we help her out?"

Rosie held back her jealousy, remembering their vow of equality.

"You're right. Remember Angelique. Well, she wrote me a letter. She likes the school in Vermont. And she says she can't wait to get back to town. But it'll only be for a short break. Summer school is tough going but she had to make up the credits she lost last year, during all that mess."

They'd become very fond of Angelique Salerno, the daughter of the murdered couple found without hands, during their last caper.

"It's nice having Angelique in our lives. It's like having a grown-up daughter," Rick said.

"We're too young to have a grown-up daughter," Rosie laughed.

"Ice wants to come to see you. She called this morning. Is it okay?"

"Tell her to come tomorrow. Mom won't be here at lunch. She has to hostess the bridge game and I told her not to worry. I'm going to be home soon. She can cook for me there. Tell Ice to come about noon."

"I love you, Rosie," Rick said, kissing her again.

Ice arrived at noon the next day, holding a bunch of daisies. When she entered the room, Rosie smiled at her warmly.

"It's nice of you to come and see me, Ice."

"Rick said you got beat up because of Baby Sue and I felt a little responsible. I should have told you that she knew a lot of weirdos."

"You did. Rick's checking out the location of the Elephant Man. He might be involved, somehow. But I was attacked by a woman."

"I'm sorry."

The nurse took the daisies and announced she was taking her lunch break. Ice relaxed, not feeling comfortable with the somber woman in the room.

"Sit here, Ice," Rosie motioned to a chair near the bed. "You know we all have our bad times. Rick tells me you're having a bad time now."

Ice nodded.

"Rick and I have had our ups and downs."

"Tell me about you and Rick."

"Well, we went steady during high school. Then we lived in sin. We were very happy."

Ice nodded.

"Then Rick went off and married someone else."

Ice's eyes opened wide.

"You're kidding."

"No, I'm not," Rosie said sadly.

"What did you do?"

"I felt just like ice," Rosie said pointedly. "I worked like a dog all week long and didn't talk to anyone. I was writing my first novel at the time. My family wasn't speaking to me because I was living in sin so I didn't want to tell them he left me. But they found out. And they kept asking me to come back home. But I couldn't. I was doing weird things."

"What kind of things?"

"I missed him most on the weekends. We used to do stupid things. We were silly and ordinary. We'd go to D'Agostino's for our Saturday night treat. We couldn't afford to eat out so we'd get those little canned mussels. That would be our extravagance. I was working for a movie company, doing public relations and writing my novel during lunch. Rick was a stringer for the *Village Voice*, writing sports articles. We were happy but broke."

She paused, gasping for breath.

"Afterwards, we'd come home to that railroad apartment. We had two rooms and thought it was a palace. Then I'd mix the chopped meat with onions, garlic and cheese, my special meatballs. We'd take out the mussels and put them on a platter my grandmother left me. Italian china makes everything elegant. Then I'd put something silky on and we'd lay on pillows on the floor and indulge. God, we were happy."

"And after he married?"

"I began going to Bergdorf Goodman Fur Salon every Saturday morning. All the women had French accents, and the salesmen were nice and I'd try on the latest minks for women who had everything. I'd try one on, and give it back. Then I'd ask for it again as if I was trying to decide whether to buy it. Hanging around the fur salon kept me excited, especially when someone tried on sable. Sable is my favorite fur."

Rosie's eyes opened wide. There was an intense fire burning in them as she remembered.

"But I wouldn't know what to do after I left the store. One day, a saleswoman said, why don't we go across to the Plaza and have a drink in that clubby bar. So one thing led to another and we met two visiting businessmen who wanted to go to a nightclub. We dropped them as soon as we were safe inside Club 54. Then I met a mechanic. I like earthy types." She laughed. "This guy said, I know a slam club in SoHo. I'd never been to one though I'd been born in SoHo. So we went there, but when we got there, I said, no, I'll get black and blue and we left."

"I used to go to slam clubs," Ice said. "Maybe I was there."

"You were about ten years old at that time."

"I got around."

"Well, we went home and made it. Right afterwards, he jumped out of bed and headed for the john. I saw him pick up a bag so I followed him. The door never really shut all the way so I could see what he was up to. He was washing himself down with a stiff brush. Guess what. He was using black soap."

Rosie started to tremble.

"I screamed. He was the first guy I made it with. Before that, it was only Rick. And then, this guy is crazy. He came out of the john looking like a naughty boy and apologized. He said there was so much disease around that he carried a kit with him. Black soap. Two stiff brushes. Rubbing alcohol. He put on his clothes and left. Before he went, he said it had nothing to do with me."

"He was right. There is a lot of disease around."

"None of that had anything to do with my life. There I was, in love with Rick, and he was in love with someone else. He was screwing her every night and living with her. He was eating with her and laughing with her. I thought I would go mad. So, I quit my job, and stayed home and wrote all day. At night I began to fool around. I learned a lot I wish I didn't know." She smiled gently. "That's why I know a little bit about what you're going through. I've been there. Not like you, perhaps. But in a bad way. My life became very dangerous."

"What happened then?"

"One day, I ran into Rick at Macy's. He was in the bedding department looking for a bed. I was bouncing around on a round mattress. He looked down at me. Then he lay down beside me and we both cried."

"Wow!"

"I asked him about Sharon. He told me she ran off with a young German count who wanted to be a filmmaker. Then he told me he made a mistake. He was a wreck. Skin and bones. Sharon believed in lots of cocaine. Then he asked me to marry him."

"What did you do?"

"I told him he'd asked me that question before and I said yes, and he disappeared. He swore he loved me and that he had been temporarily insane."

"How long?"

"Eight years."

"And you waited for him."

"In a fashion, yes."

"Wow. True love."

"Right."

"So you married him."

"He said he had a trust fund and wanted to support me. I told him I didn't care about money. Then he said he'd sign a contract saying that he had to do all the housework. He said he'd also sign a contract saying he would never leave me. I laughed. I never could resist Rick."

"He's nice."

"You like him, don't you, Ice?"

Ice lowered her eyes.

"Hey, it's okay to like him. There's a lot of ways to love men, Ice. They don't have to be sexual."

"Rick said that."

"Oh, he did."

"Yeah, he said that you and he want to be my friends."

"He's right."

"I don't know if I can be a friend to a man."

"Sure, you can, it's easy. They're human beings, you know."

"But . . ."

"I know, it's scary. Look, I lived through eight years of hell because of Rick. When he swore he would never do anything to hurt me again, I believed him. But sometimes, I still get scared. After all, someone else could come along and then, poof. Ice, it's dangerous to love somebody."

"I don't know about love, Rosie. I just know that every guy wants something from me and it's not love. Men are weird. I mean, most men."

Rosie laughed.

"Then, you've got to meet a Torrid Tarzan."

"What's that?"

"A Torrid Tarzan is a man who does not give his real name to a woman while he performs sexual feats of great eroticism causing her to orgasm several hundred times."

"Sounds like me," Ice laughed.

"All kidding aside, Ice," Rosie said. "You've got to change your life."

"Any ideas how?"

"You can sing. Why don't you record a few songs? Make a video."

"Think I could?"

"Why not? Rick and I can help."

"Would you?"

"Sure. We'd love to."

21

In the predawn darkness, the waterfront was bleak. As the water crashed against wooden planks deteriorated from neglect, the Leather Man snarled. At his feet were the bodies of three girls, hands and feet handcuffed, eyes closed, ready for the Hudson River.

A flash of regret immobilized him as he remembered their pleas for life. He'd intended to free them after they finally agreed to do his bidding. But something snapped. He'd lost his head. When the blurry mist lifted, he realized he'd killed them.

At first, he panicked. Then, shrugging away his fears, he laughed. There were plenty more where they came from, a never-ending supply of girls.

Quickly, the man pulled the bodies to the edge of the waterfront. Located near the West Side Highway, the place had been a haven for lovers who wanted complete privacy. Now, it was dangerous; a place to avoid at darkness.

Large pieces of driftwood floated by, pieces of the eroding waterfront up and down the Hudson River. There was talk that the politicians were going to refurbish this area in their quest for favors from the real estate lobby. He laughed. What would the city be without its depressed areas, its frightening locales, its neglected streets?

He tied the girls together with a strong nylon rope, at the waist, and at the feet. He added a heavy weight and then threw them into the dark cold water.

A cat screamed. The man listened. The ferocious snarls were familiar to him. A street cat wailing at his mate. The man knew about those screams. They were like the screams of a madman who killed.

He bent his head suddenly. Those poor girls. He tried to discipline them, tried to instruct them that their lives would be worth nothing if they refused his demands. In the end, they'd pleaded to do his bidding but, by that time, the fun was over for him. They'd taken too long. He was running out of patience.

Bains didn't care how he managed his crop of girls. Bains was only interested in the end results. Well, these three had not worked out. So they would disappear. It was easy. It had happened many times before.

The Leather Man watched the bodies submerge into the Hudson River. After a while, he rose, walked to his van and drove away.

22

Ice held the Capezio bag tightly to her chest. She was riding the Number Five bus, which left Washington Square Park and wound its way up to the West Side, stopping close to Felicia House. Before she left the Village she'd spent her last fifty dollars on a pair of new shoes for Tessa. She knew her sister would love the pretty white shoes with the butterfly design on the toes. Though the shoes were expensive, Ice felt like spoiling Tessa.

As the bus weaved its way up Riverside Drive, Ice made plans. She'd earn one thousand dollars for her work on the porno movie. The Leather Man was eager for her to perform and she'd bargained him from five hundred to one thousand because of his interest. By the end of the week, she could get Tessa and leave the city. Then they had to get out of the reach of the authorities. Maybe the Ramseys would help find a safe place.

Ice knew she had to save Tessa, who was too innocent for city life. Nor was Tessa strong enough to survive with Linda and her boyfriend. No, it was up to Ice to create a safe environment for Tessa; a nice place to live and grow. Where was not important, as long as it was safe.

When she reached Felicia House, the girl who answered the door told Ice to go to the director's office.

"He wants to speak to you. Wait here," she said.

Carl Collier came out of his office, bustling with careful questions.

"You're here to visit your sister?" he inquired. "When was the last time you visited her?"

Ice noticed he was very nervous. Something must have happened.

"Is she sick?"

"No, but I'm afraid she's left."

"Left? But Tessa wouldn't leave without telling me."

"I am sorry. You see, three girls ran away last night. We've called the police. You can check with them."

"I don't believe you," Ice glared at him.

Then she saw a strange glint in his eyes which did not match his conservative appearance.

"Sorry. If there's anything we can do, please call us," he said dismissing her.

Outside, in a public phone booth, Ice phoned Rick. After hearing her story, he said he'd phone his aunt to check up on Collier. Ice caught the Seventh Avenue Express subway downtown. Known in the city as the "beast," the train was filled with teenagers cruising for victims. One look at Ice told them to leave her alone.

She left the train at Sheridan Square. Swiftly she walked to Rick's loft.

Meanwhile, Rick had phoned his aunt. At his request, she'd phoned Collier about the girls' disappearance. Then she phoned Rick, to confirm that yes, the girls had left. There were no guards at Felicia House. The girls were trusted. Mandy added that Collier seemed devastated by this disappearance.

Then Rick called Kushel.

"How old was the girl?"

"Fifteen or sixteen."

"The others?"

"A little older."

"Well, I hate to tell you this, Rick, but we've fished three bodies from the river. They were mutilated like Baby Sue was."

"Oh, no."

"We figure they were murdered someplace else and dumped in the river. They got stuck on a large piece of driftwood and someone spotted them. I got the report only a half-hour ago. It's the same m.o. as Baby Sue."

"You mean . . ."

"Yup. These kids had no breasts either."

"Damn."

"We're sending a couple of detectives up to Felicia House to check out the other girls. Maybe they know something."

"My aunt runs that place. I'm sure everything is above board. Her director, Carl Collier, has excellent credentials."

"Well, it's simply a matter of form. We have to look at all angles. But it does seem that we have a ritualized killer on our hands."

"I feel responsible. I arranged for the missing girl to go to Felicia House. I thought she'd be safe there."

"Well, she may not be one of the girls, Rick."

"I hope not."

"There's only one way to find out."

"What's that?"

"Her sister will have to go to the morgue."

After Kushel hung up, Rick paced Woolfe's Lair. He wished Rosie were here. How could he tell Ice the horrible news that her sister might be dead? Rosie would know how to handle this situation. But Rosie was at the physical therapist, getting her bruised body back in shape.

Rick felt awful. How could he explain to Ice why Felicia House had not protected Tessa?

When Ice phoned at the corner phone booth, Rick said he'd come downstairs to get her. In the doorway, she demanded to know what his aunt had told him.

"My aunt confirmed Collier's story," he explained. "But

Ice, I've got bad news. The cops say that they found the bodies of three young girls. They're at the morgue. I'll go down with you."

"No, I'll go alone," Ice said, clutching the Capezio bag to her breast.

"But . . ."

"I don't want you to be involved."

"But I am involved."

"No, I'll take care of this."

She whirled about quickly, flagging a cab. When she arrived at the city morgue, she told the clerk she was there to see the three bodies found this morning.

"This way, Miss," the white-frocked man said.

Ice steeled herself as she followed him down the long corridor to a large room filled with tables. On each table, under a sheet, was a body.

"Are you going to be okay?" he asked.

"Yes."

He checked the tag on the toe of the first body. "Jane Doe Number One," he announced. Then he lifted the sheet.

Ice looked at the red-haired girl. No, it was not Tessa. She shook her head.

"Jane Doe Number Two," he said, lifting the sheet on the next table.

Ice flinched as an enormous pain erupted deep inside of her. She gripped the edge of the table. Then she noticed the bruises on her sister's body and the breast mutilation.

Ice swore.

"Is that her?" the man asked.

"Yes."

Ice dropped the Capezio bag. It crashed to the floor and she stared at it dumbly.

"Are you alright?"

"Yes, I'm fine," she answered in a steely voice.

He picked up the package and handed it to Ice, but she waved it away.

"Is this your sister?"

"Yes, it's Tessa," Ice said coldly.

23

Ice was weeping. Her basement apartment was gray though the afternoon sunlight shone brightly outside. The bars on the window reflected on the bare wooden floor, confirming the place was a jail cell.

Ice was in a prison of her own making. She sat on a beat-up gray sofa, opposite an orange chair. It was an ordinary chair with a straw matting seat. She'd found it on East First Street one morning and carried it home. Then she'd painted it orange in a mood of joy.

That day, her life seemed to be going well. She was a star at the Snake Club. She'd thought things were going to work out. But she should have known better.

Was this life? If it was, then why feel anything? Look at the mess she was in. She was going to rescue Tessa and all she did was to quicken her death. How had this happened? Her young sister was not the kind to run away. Maybe she would have been better off with Linda? No, Ice thought. Their mother would have stood by and watched Tessa ruined, the way she had with Ice.

Maybe one of the other girls convinced Tessa to flee. But Ice was sure that if Tessa had gone, she would have come to the basement. Where else would she go?

She felt desperately lonely, a feeling she hadn't had for sometime. She turned on the TV, watched a video and began to dance with herself, the way she used to in the old days, before she was a star. She'd go out each night for no reason. She wasn't interested in guys, drugs, or drinks, but simply wanted to be out there in the dark gray world of the Lower East Side. She loved the black smoke, the guttural sounds from the videos, the rich runaways, the bored uptown types who arrived in limousines, the jaded SoHoites who needed new thrills. They came to the clubs and looked for excitement. Ice sat in a corner, alone, watching them. Her attitude dared people to say hello. She didn't relate to the other girls because they were silly and talked about what was in, and who they made it with the night before. The guys competed for the girls. It was razzle-dazzle time, only Ice felt none of the dazzle.

That had been her life up to the time she became a star. Stardom had changed everything for her. After she was a star, everyone left her alone. That was the good thing about being famous, though the fame extended only to a three-block radius on the Lower East Side. People respected her. She did not have to do anything; they loved her act, loved her trash, loved Ice Goddess.

Dramatically, she danced in front of the large mirror propped against a wall. The basement apartment was one very long room. Formerly a home for rats and spidery creatures, it had been rented to Ice for only $300 per month. The landlord had told her it was safe because the bars in the windows could not be cut. Also, the double lock on the door had never been busted. Ice moved in, realizing that the basement was part of the city's underground life, like she was. She felt right at home.

Fastidious, she cleaned up the place and placed rat poison to discourage the former tenants. Then she fixed it up. She painted one wall silver and had pasted little silver stars on it like a permanent Christmas tree. The other walls were white.

On them Ice placed photographs of her favorite video stars, Prince, Michael Jackson, Madonna.

There was a bed, a couch and two armchairs. And the orange chair. In one corner, Ice had built a wall-to-wall closet for costumes. She felt like a cabaret performer because the basement doubled as a dressing room. Ice simply transported herself from one personality to another. Which one was really Ice? Was she the girl who lay in bed, reading books stored in milk cartons, turning pages to find out something about life she may not know?

Ice staggered with exhaustion and collapsed on the couch. Her eyes were teary. She couldn't turn off her faucet. She never remembered crying like this. But she did remember the sick feeling in the pit of her stomach, a raw pain.

After a while, Ice opened her eyes. The room glowed through the mist of her tears. The orange chair looked iridescent. Had she taken drugs? No. This must be a natural hallucination.

The chair glowed. Then, Ice realized it wasn't the chair but someone sitting in it. She couldn't see what he was wearing. He didn't speak or gesture but simply sat there, looking at her.

She never saw anyone who looked like him. He was beautiful. His hair was long, and not spiked. His skin looked like a young boy's. His eyes were deep blue. She opened her eyes wider, trying to see him clearly but he was like a cloud.

She knew she'd never met him because he wasn't wearing earrings or rings, and he wasn't one of those swells who came to the club to see her.

Had she picked him up?

Had he come through the door?

Was he a thief?

He looked at Ice, his blue eyes weary with ancient memories.

Then he gestured.

Ice felt odd. She was consumed with excruciating pain. Somewhere, deep inside her soul, terror was boiling. The vision gestured again and her pain turned to tears. Ice cried for an eternity. When it ended, his tender smile filled her with a strange feeling of warmth, as if he'd gone through her insides and purged all of the bad stuff.

Ice felt pure. Ivory Snow white.

She turned to thank him but he was fading.

"No," she shrieked.

She ran to the orange chair but nothing or no one was there.

A strange melody filled her head. She picked up the tape recorder she used to write her songs. She began to hum. Then the hums became a loud chorus. Then words came as she created a song about love and loss.

24

Rick held out the long black Cartier box.

"A bribe?" Rosie asked.

"For valor, above and beyond," he replied, kissing her.

She was sitting in Woolfe's Lair, surrounded by the research team's clipping on the most gruesome murders committed in the U.S. in the last ten years.

Rosie's theory was that the Viking woman was a product of Germany. Because of her Wagnerian appearance, Rosie concluded the Viking had been weaned on Nietzsche and the philosophy of the superman and superwoman. Rosie understood this philosophy and often stated that she was thankful Roman blood ran through her veins. If she'd been German, she would have been impossible.

Rosie estimated the Viking would be about fifty years old, explaining that the attacker had been in excellent physical condition due to the superwoman motif and the fact that she probably ate nothing but greens and worked out at her local health club. She could also have been an Olympic champ or a professional wrestler in her country. And, to conclude, Rosie was sure that the Viking had been here less than a dozen years.

"How did you come to these conclusions?" Rick asked, when informed of Rosie's thesis.

"Well, if she was six years old in nineteen-thirty-nine when World War II and Nazism was in full bloom, than she was spoon fed the Hitler philosophy and as we know, what happens to us before we are five controls our entire life on this planet Earth."

"Nothing happened to me before I was five," Rick said.

"See what I mean."

He laughed.

"Okay, okay, go on with your logic."

"Well, I think she was a teenager during the postwar period when Germany was overrun by Americans and Russians. That probably made her mad. She probably emigrated to France when she was twenty-one because Germany was boring, nothing but industry and Cold War." She gasped for breath. "And, in France, she probably was a Cabaret performer or a wrestler or both."

"When was she in the Olympics?"

Rosie frowned.

"I don't think she ever was but she could have been."

"How do you know she left Germany?"

"By the way she talked on the phone. She definitely had an European rather than a German accent. And her voice was trained. If she was an Olympic champ, her voice would not have been worked on."

"True."

"Then, I think at some point, France lost its charm and she came to America."

"Maybe not. Why not England?"

"Because, if she'd gone to England instead of France, she still would be living there. Germans love the fog. It's gloomy and suits their personalities."

"I see."

"So, it must have been France. Germans think the French are frivolous, but how much fun can a German take?"

"Not much, apparently. You don't like them much, do you?"

Her eyes shot open.

"Why, I love Wagner. He's my very favorite composer. All that passion. All that sweat and suffering. But, though I like his music, I do think he's a bit hard on the human race. Italians," she concluded, "have more compassion."

"Ever read *Death in Venice?*"

"Five times," she snapped. "But writers are compassionate, Rick, whomever they are. It's what they have in common."

"Okay, Okay," Rick agreed, worn out by Rosie's illogical onslaught on his logical senses. Besides, he knew from past experience that though Rosie sounded as if she didn't know what she was talking about, often she was right. She had a strange intuition he didn't have. Neither did most of the world.

She turned the black box over in her hands.

"Open it," Rick suggested.

"Right."

When she did, Rosie gasped. Inside the box was a heart of rubies on a gold chain.

"Rick, it's gorgeous."

"I know you hate expensive jewelry but I want you to have this."

"I'll wear it everywhere."

"Not in New York, you won't."

"I'll wear it under a scarf. Muggers won't know."

"You'll wear it when I'm with you and not any other time. Don't ask for trouble."

She sparkled.

"You sound like my dad," she laughed. "After all these years, you're becoming Italian by osmosis."

"You got to me years ago," he jumped on her, messing the clippings piled on the floor.

"Let me put this on," he said.

"It still hurts."

He kissed the bruises on her neck.

"Darling, I'm sorry."

"Just part of our job."

"We'll save the heart for when you're healed."

Then he held her close.

She'd been home from the hospital for a few days but instead of sitting in bed and doing nothing, as she was told, Rosie immediately began working on the book. Because her doctor had instructed her to relax, eat good food, and watch game shows, Rosie swore Rick to secrecy. To do nothing was death to his Rosie. So they compromised. He'd set up a quasi-bed on the couch in Woolfe's Lair and every day Celia delivered home-cooked food for her daughter. But, though Rosie insisted that her portable typewriter be near, Rick informed her in no uncertain terms that if he caught her typing he would personally kill her with his bare hands.

"Enough is enough," he said. "Stop being a workaholic."

"One of us has to."

"Why?"

"To pay the rent."

"We could swim for the rest of our lives and our rent would be covered."

"Have we good investments?"

"The best."

She smiled.

"You WASPS are smart. Italians spend their money foolishly."

"We have foolish money, too."

"Do we?"

"How about that villa in Italy?"

"Next year. After we clean up this messy Baby Sue case, we'll take a trip. You'll drive. I'll sit in the back seat. Okay?"

"Hey, that's no fun. We'll hire a driver."

"Neat."

She was dressed in blue silky Baby Dolls. Low cut, they were trimmed in antique lace.

Rick nuzzled the lace.

"Red rubies for Aries," she said, looking at the heart.
"I thought diamonds were your birthstone."
"Rubies suit us. Hot fire."
"I bought rubies because I want you to know how I feel about you, darling."
"How's that, fella?"
"Deep."
Her eyes grew teary and she reached for him. Holding him close to her heart, she hummed a sweet tune. After a while, she said, "Do you know the three things human beings need for survival, darling?"
"Tell me."
"Food, shelter, and affection."
"How do you know that?"
"It's in my survival file. It's interesting that it isn't sex, but affection that keeps us alive."
"Isn't sex affectionate?"
"Not for everyone. Those teenage girls are being used sexually but there's no affection there."
"True."
"Sex and hate get all mixed up. We're a puritan country and that means sex is considered dirty."
"I like it."
"I hope you will always like it," she laughed. "There's a new study. Do you know that the majority of women polled said they prefer affection to sex?"
"What does that mean?"
"It means that women aren't getting enough affection." She paused thoughtfully. "Think of Ice. She's had a lot of sex in her life. But how much affection has she had? Almost none it seems."
"Poor kid."
"You like her, don't you?"
"She's like you, brave. She wouldn't let me go to the morgue. Kushel said she didn't crack a tear. The clerk called him and ran down the whole thing."
"She probably cried when she was alone."

"Maybe."

"Ice adores you, Rick."

"I don't know . . ."

"She doesn't know how to act with you. Men always hit on her sexually. You don't. She's not used to that."

"Men are bastards," he said.

"Only some," she agreed. "These men who can murder women they've made love to . . . it seems to me that after you make love to someone, they're special. How can you kill a person after you've shared that?"

Rick thought for a moment.

"I don't think men make love with their brains. I didn't like Sharon very much, but I wanted to have sex with her."

Rosie looked pained at the mention of his first wife.

"Rick, did you run away from me because we were used to each other?"

"Nope. That wasn't it."

"Do you know why?"

"I think it was because we were too close."

"Too close?"

"Uh, huh. Most people put a reserve on their love. I mean, where I grew up, I never knew who cared for whom. Nobody showed feelings. Then I met you. I guess I ran scared after a while. I guess I thought that I couldn't be that close to anyone."

"And now?"

"Now I think I'm the luckiest man in the world."

Later, the phone rang and Rosie insisted they answer it because they were expecting a call from the West Coast.

"Hello," Rick said.

It was Kushel telling Rick that the police had picked up the Elephant Man on the beach in Malibu where he was pretending to be an independent movie producer. They'd identified him because at a local cocaine party he'd done an excellent imitation of an elephant. A police informer (cocaine parties were filled with them) had filed a report on this strange occurrence and Kushel, ever observant, had read the report and phoned the West Coast immediately.

"But that doesn't mean the guy will talk," he warned Rick.

"We'll sic Mario on him," Rick suggested.

"Why are you talking about my dad to that cop?" Rosie interrupted.

"No Italian stuff. I know who sent those gray dogs down to the Snake Club. Don't you, Rick?" Kushel said.

"What's he saying about my dad?" Rosie insisted.

"Look, no one was hurt, Kush," Rick said into the phone, waving Rosie away, "But Italians have to stop this kind of thing."

"Why?" Kushel asked.

"If they don't, who will?"

"The police. That's our job."

"Then do it."

"When the Elephant Man gets to New York I'll let you question him. You'll see how easy it is to break down a criminal."

"Hey, Kush, I didn't mean to insult you."

"Insult him. Insult him," Rosie whispered into Rick's ear.

"He's coming back voluntarily," Kushel boasted.

"How did you manage that?"

Kushel laughed.

"We got our ways," he answered. "Good-bye."

Rick hung up.

"So?" Rosie asked.

"Elephant Man has been found in Malibu and he's coming back to New York voluntarily."

"How did Kushel manage that?"

"He won't say."

"Everybody's an Italian." she laughed.

"Hey, what's that?"

Rick started for the elevator door because strange sounds were coming from it, and in New York City that meant trouble. Suddenly, without warning, the elevator door swung open and three gypsy violinists appeared, playing wildly. Behind them, Miles Hamilton, their literary agent and friend, held a large bouquet of pink tea roses.

"For you, my dearest," he said to Rosie.

"Miles, how did you get up here?" Rick asked, worried about security.

"Arnoldo let me in. I phoned him. I wanted to surprise you."

The violinists surrounded Rosie, playing passionately. Then three waiters arrived, carrying large picnic baskets filled with caviar, cheeses, bottles of French champagne.

"A party!" Rosie exclaimed, clapping her hands. "What's it for?"

"*SoHo Vice* is wrapped. They're editing it and I understand the rushes are marvelous. Stu Vesco knows what he's doing."

"We haven't heard a word from our producer," Rosie complained.

"Bains is a strange one. He lives like a recluse between pictures. He likes to think he's Howard Hughes."

"Ugh!" Rosie made a face. Then she jumped up and began dancing around the room. The violinists and the waiters eyed her seminude outfit with delight.

Rick ushered Miles's staff to the elevator. "It'll take you down," he said, handing them five-dollar tips. "Thank you."

When the elevator door slammed shut, he turned.

"Rosie, put clothes on."

"Oh, Miles isn't embarassed."

"But I am."

He opened the door to her closet and picked a pink and blue negligee.

"Here," he said pointedly.

"My husband's a puritan," she said to Miles, putting on the negligee.

"I know." Miles laughed. "That's why you make such a good team."

"Oh?" Rick felt antsy.

"Pagan and puritan," Miles chuckled. "Rick, back off. You know I love you and Rosie."

"She's supposed to be convalescing. Look at her."

Rosie was dancing around Woolfe's Lair, touching everything, and finally jumping up on the piano keys where she proceeded to play a strange melody with her feet.

"Have a glass of champagne," Miles urged.

"Oh, fame, fame, fame, how I love you," she sang. Then she jumped back down from the piano and ran over to Rick. "Rick," she said, climbing onto his lap. "We're finally in the movie business."

25

"*Come on*, Ice, baby, let's see what you got," Leather Man taunted.

He was standing behind the cameraman, cueing Ice for her porno debut.

Ice was lying on a round bed covered with blue satin, trying to remember the one thousand dollars that she'd receive for the film. The end justifies the means, she thought. Be impersonal. Be Ice. You're an unthinking, unfeeling body.

She tried to retain these thoughts as her muscular costar, George, made love to her before the camera.

"Hurry up," she urged.

"I'm supposed to keep you suspended," he complained.

His eyes were dead. Ice guessed he'd done cocaine to get ready for his role.

As hours passed, Ice felt sicker. While trashing her life and body at the Snake Club exhilarated her, vulgarizing herself in front of a camera did not. Finally, she decided nothing was worth this humiliation.

"Okay, let's can it," she said, getting up from the bed.

"We're not finished," the cameraman complained.

"You're finished, dude," she said, wrapping a robe around her body.

Leather Man went to her side, his steely eyes glaring from behind his mask.

"We need more footage," he insisted.

"No more," she said. "You got enough for two films."

Her co-star stared at her stupidly, a look she'd seen on the faces of street prostitutes.

This was all downhill, Ice thought. Got to get out of here quick.

"I'm going," she stated.

"But you gotta see the man."

"What man?"

Ice was getting into her polka-dot frock, dark blue with white dots. She put on an old-fashioned straw hat with fake plastic strawberries on the rim. Then she slid into her buckle-up red boots and piled on necklaces of red beads.

"This way," Leather Man said.

"I said I'm finished."

"The main man has your cash."

Shrugging her shoulders, she followed him through a doorway. On the other side was a luxurious room. Ice reacted. This was a set up. No, she wasn't going to play party girl.

Bains had been watching the filming. The girl was all steel. He liked that. Too many young girls caved in under pressure from Leather Man. He changed quickly because he was sweaty from his erotic thoughts. Now he stood in the center of the room, dressed in a long black velvet robe. Under the robe, he wore only three gold chains around his neck.

"This is your boss, Ice," Leather Man said.

"You were simply wonderful," Bains complimented.

"What's wonderful about a dirty movie?" Ice replied sarcastically.

Bains signalled Leather Man to leave. Then, he put his arm around Ice, but she shrugged him away.

"You got my loot?"

"I thought we'd celebrate. Champagne?" he offered. "Caviar?"

"Don't have the time."

He laughed.

"We must talk about your future."

"Got no future," she said sullenly.

"Now, why don't you relax?"

"Look, Mister Moneyman, give me my thousand bucks. Okay?"

He laughed and handed her an envelope stuffed with cash.

"I can't believe you're not excited about your film debut . . ." he began.

"Excited? Listen, my man. I don't get excited. You understand," Ice said, her steely eyes sending him a message that sent exciting shivers up and down his spine.

Casually, she counted the money.

"It's all there," he said, feeling his body tremble.

This teenager was afraid of nothing. Leather Man had told him about Ice but Bains didn't believe it. Well, he'd find a way to get to her. He licked his lips in anticipation.

"How about a kiss for papa," he suggested.

She stuffed the envelope into her bag.

"You ain't my papa, Mr. Film Producer," she sangsong. "Now, how do I get out of this dump?"

26

Amanda had finished her leisurely brunch and was settling into her favorite escape, a mystery novel. She was deep into the novel when Grooms interrupted her.

"There's a messenger who needs your personal signature, madam."

"I don't expect anything. Who's it from?"

"There isn't any return address."

"Oh, very well."

Amanda walked into the hall where a special delivery man was waiting.

"Sign please," he said.

She signed and thanked him. Then she looked at a large can of film.

"I wonder who it's from?"

"Shall we screen it, Madam?"

"Yes, please."

Amanda's library doubled as a small screening room. Often, she watched her favorite films in the evening. Grooms put the film in the machine and turned the lights off.

The film began; it was a very old print. Then she saw Felicia. She watched for a few minutes, then signalled Grooms.

"Please turn this off," she said hastily.

When the phone rang, she knew what was going to happen.

"Mrs. Lord," the gruff voice said.

"Yes."

"You got our package?"

"Yes."

"Now, we have copies of this special art film. But we'll keep them private if you cooperate."

"What do you want?"

"Your nephew, Ramsey, is too smart. We want you to get him to drop his latest caper. Do you understand what we mean?"

"I don't know whether Rick will do that."

"I think you can convince him. If you can't, we're going to send this film around to every porno theater in the country."

Then the caller hung up.

Amanda deliberated about what she should do. If she called the police, headlines were sure to follow. Finally, she called Mario.

"What can I do for you?" Mario asked gallantly, sensing Amanda's disquiet.

"I need your help."

"Anything. After all, you're family."

"Can you come up to the penthouse?"

"Be right there."

True to his word, Mario arrived within the half-hour. He was wearing a white safari suit and looked out of place in the elegant rococo setting. When he entered the library, Amanda began sneezing.

"Still got that cold," he noted.

Amanda relaxed.

"Mario, someone has threatened Rick."

"Who did that?"

"Don't know. You see, they sent me a copy of a film Felicia Montremart made when she was very young."

"She was very beautiful."

"Yes, unfortunately, this is what we call an X-rated film."

"Oh. Too bad."

"Well, for years, she did everything she could to destroy prints of that film. But, obviously, someone has private stock."

"But she's dead, Amanda. What's the point? Does she have children?"

"No. But it's Felicia House. I dedicated it to her. I wouldn't want the girls to think badly of Felicia."

"I understand. She was your friend."

"Yes, my only friend."

"Too bad," Mario said. "But then good friends are hard to find, aren't they, Amanda?"

"Yes," she agreed.

"Didn't she kill herself?"

"They think she did. She wrote me a letter the day before and sounded desperate. But nobody knows what happened because her villa caught fire and everything was burned beyond recognition. There were human bones in the refuse, which they assumed were Felicia's and her staff's."

"She shouldn't have killed herself," Mario said, blessed himself quickly.

"I know."

"That's giving up. We should never give up. Nobody told us life would be easy."

"Felicia tried," Amanda said seriously. "I think she was bored. She'd always been the center of world attention. Then, as she aged, the world turned its back on her and she couldn't handle it."

"But she was a great actress."

"She didn't believe in herself. Felicia thought her fans loved her because she was beautiful. When her beauty faded, so did her self-confidence."

"Look, Amanda, there's only one thing to do. When they call again . . ."

"They didn't say they'd call again."

"They will. We'll get Kushel to put a tap on your phone."

"I didn't want to involve the police."

"I know how you feel. But in this case, I think we should."

"If you say so, Mario."

"Good. We got to do what's right. Look, don't mention this to Rick. He's got his hands full. I'll take care of things. Trust me."

"I do. Thank you."

He waved his hands at her.

"Hey, it's nothing. You can count on me."

"Mario, you're a peach."

"Hey, Amanda," he said, "know something?"

"What's that?"

"You've stopped that damned sniffling."

It had been a difficult morning for Ice. All the way out to the Long Island cemetery, she'd sat in the long black limousine hired for the funeral, silently staring out of the window. Rick and Rosie, sitting with her, had kept silent out of respect for her feelings. At the gravesite there was no ceremony. Instead, Ice played a tape of the song she'd written for Tessa. Then she'd wept.

On the return trip to the city, Rosie insisted that Ice stay at the loft for a few days. Now, still in her black threads, a long dress covered with tulle, black elfin boots, and a large black straw hat, Ice sat opposite Rosie in Woolfe's Lair.

"Look, Ice," Rosie was saying, "we've got to tell Kushel about that porno crew."

"I don't care about them."

"Rosie, leave her be," Rick interrupted.

Ice's mascara had melted in the summer heat, causing her face to look like a clown, which gave her a sadder appearance than normal.

"You two don't know anything about life," she sangsong bitterly. "You live in this beautiful loft and run around in your "Dynasty" clothes and you think you know how it is."

"Ice, don't attack us," Rick said kindly. "Remember we're your friends."

"Friends. Friends," she sangsong. Then she stopped. "You're right. You are my friends."

"We simply want to help," Rosie said softly. "You have courage. If we can close these people down..."

"You'll never stop them. More will come."

"We can try."

"Oh, try, try, try," she began stomping about the loft doing her trash act, "look, I live on the edge. When I was fifteen, I was living on the street with the clothes on my back. I couldn't handle a job. I lived on coffee for a month. I don't know why I didn't die. I slept in alleyways. I got wet. One time, it rained for four days and I was crazy. That's when I said, Ice, you gotta change your life or you're going to end up d-e-a-d. Well, I was lucky. Most girls don't change their lives on the Lower East Side. Do you know there are no women over twenty? Only the boys last. The girls fade out fast. They either graduate to uptown or they escape back home and get married. Or they die. Like Tessa," she moaned her sister's name. "Why didn't I take care of her?"

"Stop it, Ice," Rick said firmly. "You can't blame yourself. It was an accident."

"It's no accident. I should have had her with me," she stopped, suddenly dizzy.

"Ice, sit here," Rosie put her arm around the girl. "Your song to your sister was beautiful."

"My angel helped me write that song."

"Your angel?" Rick repeated.

"Yes, he appeared to me after I saw Tessa's body. He helped me. I didn't know I could love any longer, but he showed me I could."

"We'd like to help you too," Rosie said.

"Help. Help," she sangsong.

"Look, grow up," Rosie said, angrily. "Do you want to play your music and sing your songs? Well, you can do it.

You had everyone at the Snake Club mesmerized and they're the hardest people to entertain. The uptown people, the people in the suburbs, on the farms, they're easy compared to that crowd. Look, we loved your song," Rosie pointed to Rick and herself. "Do you want to give something to this life or do you want to sit around and trash everything, even Tessa's memory?"

Ice looked at Rosie with tears in her eyes.

"I want to sing," she whispered.

"Okay. Rick and I will talk to a few people. Rick, Vesco should know who can help Ice make a video, shouldn't he?"

"Right. I'll get him on the phone tomorrow morning," Rick said.

"Okay, Ice?" Rosie asked.

"Okay," Ice agreed.

The elevator door opened and the Prince robot walked out of the car and into Woolfe's Lair. Behind him, Arnoldo, dressed in soft grey flannel jumpsuit, entered. He wore an iron cross in one earlobe.

"Chuggulugg," the robot said, spying Ice.

"He's cute," Ice giggled.

"I think you've got a fan," Rosie noted.

"Chuggulgugglug," Prince said.

"He said he'd love you forever," Arnoldo explained.

Ice looked up at the electronics wizard. Then, spotting the iron cross, she laughed.

"Who are you?" she asked.

"Arnoldo is our neighbor," Rick explained. "He makes things work. Like Prince."

Ice put her arms around the robot.

"He's wonderful," she laughed.

"He knows about you," Arnoldo whispered.

"What does he know?"

"I told him what a wonderful singer you are. I used to listen to you at the Snake Club."

"You went there?"

"A few times."

Rick signalled Rosie and they disappeared into the kitchen as Arnoldo, the Prince, and Ice gossiped. When they returned with a tray of food, Arnoldo exclaimed, "Prince wants to sleep here tonight. Can he?"

"Of course," Rick agreed, knowing that the robot was Arnoldo's alter ego.

"Let's eat," Rosie urged, happy that Ice's sadness had lifted.

Later that night, in the privacy of their bedroom, Rosie threw a pillow at Rick.

"You're a matchmaker at heart," she accused him.

"So you are."

"But Arnoldo? With Ice?"

She shook her head.

"They're made for each other."

"Explain please," she insisted.

"Well, you see, Arnoldo believes in electronics and has invented the Prince to act out his libido . . . the feelings that he doesn't have when he's into S and M at the Snake Club. Understand?"

Rosie shook her head, confused. Rick was beginning to sound like her.

"Well, now that the Snake Club is closed down he's going to have to find another way to find a girl and what better way than to have his robot sleep with Ice."

"Oh, I understand that part, I mean, Arnoldo flipped over Ice. But what about Ice?"

"Ice will feel comfortable with someone gallant and who's into electronics and robots. It's what her generation cut their teeth on. Think of *Star Wars*."

"How do you know for sure?"

"Look, Rosie, if Ice met an ordinary man she'd panic. She needs someone nutty."

"But Arnoldo is crazy, Rick."

"Rosie, underneath that guise of electronic data beats a wild savage heart."

28

The grit in Ice's voice suggested years of hard living. But when she got to the chorus, her tones were strong and sure. She sang with all the gusto she could manage, singing of the innocents who were weaned, along with her, in an age of drugs and nuclear war.

"Thought I was goin' to be close to you. Thought I would care for you. I tried. I tried. I failed."

Inspired, she added some tongue-in-cheek lyrics.

"Love is the holocaust. Love is for corpses. Let's love. I want to die in your arms. I want to be buried with you forever. I cry. I tried. I cry."

In the control booth, her crew watched their goddess of alienation. In her anguish she was following the transformation jungle style of her heroes: David Bowie and Michael Jackson mixed with Prince's sexuality: the Ice Goddess, the new apostle of love and loss. Her jungle beat sounded new. It wasn't rock, or punk, or New Wave, and its electronic motif belied a definite aspect of the romantic, a belief from this young diva. Ice, dressed in a collarless white shirt over long white baggy trousers, never missed an opportunity to focus innocence on her face.

"This video is going to be sensational," the director, Juan

Klein, commented. Known for his handling of avant-garde rock stars, Klein had agreed to come to a rehearsal at Stu Vesco's request.

Rosie and Rick were seated alongside Klein.

"She's going to be a star," Rosie stated.

"She deserves a break," Rick added.

Klein laughed.

"These kids are so young and have lived so much," he commented.

Rosie and Rick suppressed a smile because Klein was about thirty and talking like an aged person. All throughout this caper, they had discussed the fact that everyone involved was younger than they were, causing them to feel like Mr. and Mrs. Grandpa and Grandma to this crew.

The orchestra, backing Ice, were all under twenty, yet their eyes had clear evidence of too much living. In the center of them, Ice was all motion now. Face to face, she sang to one musician, then another, in her easygoing manner. She held court with her quirky passion, the notes from her throat ranging over emotions which hit everyone deeply.

"It's vegetative. It's important," Klein whispered.

Rosie squeezed Rick's hand.

"We've done it," she whispered.

"Uh, huh."

"It's good to be famous," she said.

"And rich."

"Ice will find out soon."

During the days that followed, Ice worked hard, never taking breaks, showing up on time, not even taking time to smoke cigarettes, which Rosie was at her to give up. At the end of the week, she'd recorded four of her songs. One was chosen for the video, the one she'd written for Tessa. As the video process was going into full blast, Ice felt happy again.

On the set she appeared in a glittery body suit and matching laced boots, her face savagely made up. She had three sets of costumes that day. The glitter for the introductory motif. Then a soft pink chiffon trash outfit. For the end of the video, she'd selected her favorite costume: the white dotted swiss outfit she'd worn when she met Rick and Rosie.

"Low and dazzling," Klein whispered when he saw the white layers of tulle and ribbons.

"I'm exorcising my demons," she murmured.

"The camera loves you."

"I'll love it back," she laughed.

When it was over, Ice felt odd. Rosie told Ice that what was happening to her was the proof of the power of love, that her love for Tessa translated into song would change her life.

Ice didn't know whether Rosie was right, but her life was drastically changing. When she received the advance check for the video, she immediately went out to buy new clothes for her next evolution. She was hanging out at Broadway and Houston Street, in Arnoldo's large loft. She decided to change herself into a boy mentality for her new life with Arnoldo and the Prince robot. Ice created a presence so aggressive that Arnoldo and she, with their new black motorcycle and pink leather clothes, began a new trend in SoHo. To perfect her new motif, Ice dyed her blue-white hair to shocking pink because it was Arnoldo's favorite color.

Meanwhile, Rosie pursued her relentless quest for information. One morning, she and Ice had a quiet leisurely brunch while Rick was out running and Arnoldo was tinkering with a new invention.

"Rosie, do you think I could get that dirty movie killed?" Ice asked.

"Probably not. But you could stop that porno factory from operation if you'd tell us where it's located."

"Don't want you and Rick to get involved with those creeps," Ice sangsong. "Besides Arnoldo would probably blow up the place."

"Arnoldo is mad for you, isn't he?"

Rosie enjoyed the look of pleasure on Ice's face.

"We won't handle it. We'll give the information to the police."

"Ugh. Cops." Ice made a face.

"Honestly, Ice, you've got to help us. We're at a dead end. We can't find a link between Baby Sue, Hoofer Harris, Tessa's death, and those other two teenagers," Rosie stated. "There's got to be someone or something connecting that S and M crowd with the porno film people. But those porno people create dummy corporations so that it's impossible to find out who they are. If you'll simply tell us where you went to make that film, we could start there. There must be a lease on the place, or ownership papers filed someplace in the city."

"Promise you won't do anything?" Ice questioned Rosie closely because she felt responsible for Rosie's difficulty with the Viking Woman.

"I promise, Ice," Rosie said.

When the vice squad investigated the information Ice gave Rosie, they found the Ninth Avenue studio intact but no one there. After a week-long surveillance, Kushel told Rosie that he felt the studio had been abandoned by whomever was operating it. But Kushel, diligently checking through the building's ownership papers, from one dummy corporation to another, finally found out that there was a connection to Collier Films, Rosie's own producer.

"Imagine. Our very own producer was into dirty films. Ugh!" Rosie said to Rick.

"Well, producers have to start somewhere," Rick quipped.

"Huh?"

"You need a lot of talent to be a first-rate movie producer. You also need a lot of experience and not the kind that you get at Harvard Business School."

"What do you mean?"

"A porno filmmaker is the right kind of experience," Rick suggested.

"I see your ongoing hatred of Hollywood is still alive and well," Rosie laughed. Then seriously, she said, "Rick, I'm worried."

"What's the matter, my love?"

"I spoke to our agent. Miles said that Bains had disappeared. He and his partner are obviously part of this porno scandal."

"You never did like that guy."

"I know. But, Rick," she said with a savage earnestness which startled him, "this whole affair is going to hold up the release of *SoHo Vice*."

29

The Leather Man smiled as he drank his coffee. From the window of the abandoned building, he viewed a three-block radius. In most buildings, windows had fallen out of city property and boards had replaced the open spaces. The area resembled a war-torn area, his battle zone.

He chuckled. He'd been right to warn Bains that Ice might talk. Bains ordered the Leather Man to stop her but he hadn't been able to. Ice was always with someone. Her new crazy boyfriend. Those writers. Or the studio people. Before he could pop Ice, things got out of hand.

Bains was okay. He flew his private jet to Brazil where the Colonel had a welcome mat waiting. That would stop the police at Bains's door. There was no evidence connecting anyone else to the porno studio.

The Leather Man knew he was safe. Now he paced up and down the long room. With its padded walls and thick carpets, it muffled the sounds of the city.

He'd changed his disguise. On the table before him were the black leather clothes and the red mask. Now he was dressed in a conservative dark cotton running suit. There was only one reminder of his former self, his shaven head. But there were many men in Manhattan who sported this look. He didn't think he'd stand out.

He sat in front of a long mirror and began fitting plastic for his facial disguise. Over his nose he fitted an inch of the plastic which changed his fine slim nose to a pouchy one. More plastic for his cheekbones. Yes, he looked like a cheery fat fellow now, no one to worry about.

Good. He had to continue his important work, to wipe out these tribes of young girls who entered into his sphere of existence.

He was focusing his energy on one young girl in particular, relishing the various ways he would mutilate her before granting her the gift of eternal sleep.

He pressed his large hands down hard on his chest. Sometimes, when he was excited, his nipples grew taut though he knew this was anatomically impossible. For his breasts were his weak point, a result of plastic surgery, and not connected to his glands. His breathing grew frantic as he fantasized about what he would do to Ice when he caught her in his net.

30

The man was huge. When he spoke his nose seemed to dig deeply into his mouth. His first sounds sounded like a kind of grunt, then dissolved into the kind of British accent which could only have been nurtured in India. His complexion was bright pink from a sunlamp. Since he'd been at Malibu, Rick, watching, couldn't understand why the sunburn wasn't natural.

Rick studied the Elephant Man. His body was brutally muscular. When Rick had played college football, he'd been tackled by this type of body and had learned how to recognize that the layers of fat hid a brutal muscular strength.

"There's all that money in Malibu," the man was saying in a raspy thin voice. "I went to several parties for the starving babies in Africa. Lots of cocaine was served, but I dare say, everyone there seemed to be a law officer. Vice people travel in the strangest circles."

"Tell us about Baby Sue," Kushel asked.

Rick watched his police colleague who was riding on a successful crest because he'd gotten the Elephant Man to return to the city and no one knew how. Rosie, who was at home and forbidden to leave her convalescent bed, had phoned

Rick several times with the theory that Kushel had blackmailed the Elephant Man.

The man's head hung low.

"I loved Baby Sue," he said flatly.

"Were you her lover?"

"I loved her too much to use her sexually," the Elephant Man said tearfully. "I wanted to save her from that type of life. I said, Baby Sue, I got loot. I'll take you out to Malibu and introduce you to all those beautiful slim people who love to turn gorgeous young girls into stars. But she refused. She said no, she was scared. And she seemed to enjoy that S and M scene, you know."

Rick was startled at the changes in the man's accent, sometimes British, sometimes California, sometimes Lower East Side.

"Tell us about it?" Kushel continued his questioning.

"I don't know exactly how the thing works, but Baby Sue got off on getting busted in the chops. And then, there was this man . . . she called him the Leather Man."

"Who?"

"He was the middleman for whomever was paying Baby Sue. She never told me much about the Money Man except to say that he was very kinky in the sack."

"How kinky?"

"Pretty. But that was old stuff to her. She didn't talk about the Money Man much. But she did talk about this Leather Man. She said he was huge and wore leather and always hid his face behind a red mask. She never saw what he really looked like. Funny thing though, the dude never touched her. He only trained her."

"Where?"

"She told me about this place uptown. It was where they trained the girls. Some kind of house. In the basement, Baby Sue said they had a school. They taught the girls how to respond to the kinky stuff . . . you know the whips and cuffs and things like that. I don't understand all of that. But Baby Sue thought it was hot stuff. My poor girl."

His large brown eyes were teary.

"Why did you run away when she bought it?"

"I couldn't accept my feelings. I wanted to kill this man, whoever he was. I asked around the Snake Club if people knew him. I heard one night, he'd gone nuts for Ice Goddess."

Rick's ears perked up. Did Ice know this man?

"Yeah, one night he made a scene there. He swept into the place and grabbed her while his punk pals broke up the place. It became a legend at the Snake Club. Only Ice Goddess would never tell anyone what happened. When her buddies asked her about the guy, she said he was nothing. Apparently he didn't threaten Ice, but he got to Baby Sue."

Rick felt humilated. He'd thought Ice trusted him and Rosie. What would Rosie say when she heard this news?

"Do you know where this house is?"

"Not exactly, but I picked up Baby Sue a couple of times. I think I could point it out."

Suddenly, the Elephant Man began weeping.

"Oh, Baby Sue, I loved you. Why did you have to be so mad? We could have lived on a house at the beach. You could have had a suntan all year round."

"Mr. Calvin," Kushel asked, "how do you earn your money?"

The Elephant Man's name was Thomas Calvin and his birthplace was Bath, England.

"You've heard of Calvin's Chutney. Well, it's my family. But I'm not a businessman so my company is run by a board of directors. They simply send me checks, mate." He reached into his baggy pants pockets and threw several checks on the floor. "I don't know what to do with them. I can't spend it. Here. Want some?" he said to Kushel and Rick.

"I'm sure you don't want to bribe an officer of the law," Kushel said.

The pink man flushed as he hastily picked up the checks and pushed them back into his pants pockets.

"Oh, excuse me. I didn't mean that."

"Let's go," Kushel said. Then to Rick, "Want to come?"

"Absolutely. I'd better or my wife won't speak to me."

The party left in a police van because the Elephant Man could not easily sit in a police car. There was Rick, Kushel, the prisoner, and two police guards.

As the car sped uptown, Rick had the sinking sensation that it would reach its destination at Felicia House. It made perfect sense. Somehow, there was a connection. Baby Sue had been found in Aunt Mandy's basement. Tessa and the other two teenagers, had been staying there, and had been found murdered. Rick worried that somehow his aunt would be brought into this awful mess.

"Take Riverside Drive," the Elephant Man instructed, "and drive slow."

At 110th Street, Rick knew for sure. When Felicia House came into view, Thomas Calvin shouted.

"That's it. The house on the corner."

"Isn't that your aunt's—" Kushel began.

"Yes, Kush." Rick interrupted him.

The girl who answered the door was a teenager, dressed in a schoolgirl's pleated skirt and high collared shirt.

"Yes?" she said.

"Police."

Kushel showed her a search warrant.

"Oh. You have to see Dr. Collier," she said, too frightened for a schoolgirl.

"We'll talk to him later. Take the upstairs," Kushel said to one cop. "Come on, Rick, we'll go downstairs. You," he pointed to the second cop, "stay with Mr. Calvin."

They walked toward the rear of the elegant lobby. From the rear dining room, a staircase wound its way to the basement of the house. Kushel turned on his flashlight as he and Rick descended the steep stairs.

"Jesus!" Kushel cursed. Then he turned on a light switch.

Before them was a dungeon, outfitted with a wall of paraphernalia. Cuffs for wrists, necks, and ankles hung in a display. An assortment of heavy to light whips. Leather belts, boots, pants, shorts lay in a pile.

"It's an S and M dungeon," Kushel observed.

"Aunt Mandy is going to go into shock."

"Your aunt seems to go in and out of this thing," Kushel said harshly. "Baby Sue was found in her basement. Then the film of Felicia Montremart."

"What film?"

"Oh, yeah, you don't know. Your father-in-law asked me to tap your aunt's phone. Some dirty film collector sent her a copy of a dirty film starring Felicia Montremart."

"She was my godmother," Rick said.

"Really? Well, the caller said that he'd expose the film in this country if your aunt didn't get you to stop this investigation."

"Nobody told me."

"Mario didn't want to worry you. Rosie had just been hurt and he thought you had enough on your mind. But this means there is some kind of link between your aunt and all this."

"Kush, my aunt is above suspicion."

"Nobody's above suspicion, not even you."

"Maybe Dr. Collier can explain."

"Let's go talk to him."

Upstairs, in his office, Carl Collier looked faint.

"Can you tell us about that place downstairs?" Kushel asked.

"It was my brother. He forced me."

"Forced you to do what?"

"I told them it was wrong but they wouldn't listen. I tried to help the girls afterwards. I'd give them therapy."

"Some therapy," Kushel said harshly.

"My brother always made me do things I didn't want to do."

"The films?"

"Yes, my brother is Chad Collier. He's president of Collier Films. His partner, Bains, made those films using the girls. Chad told me not to think about it."

"What about the man in leather?" Kushel asked.

Collier looked frightened.

"I can't talk about him."

"You'd better."

"I don't know who he is. He would appear and disappear. I never saw his face."

"How did you contact him?"

"I never did anything. Bains would call and tell me when the man was coming for a certain girl. I never knew anything more than that."

"Did he come for Tessa Martin?" Rick asked grimly.

"Yes. And we never saw her again. She was so nice."

"Do you know what happened?"

"No. I only know that sometimes he got mad when a girl wouldn't obey him. And when he was mad, he was dangerous."

"What's the connection with my aunt?" Rick said.

Collier shook his head nervously.

"He always asked questions about Mrs. Lord. What she was doing? How she looked? I don't know how he got into her basement but he's very clever. He could get through any locks or gates."

"So he left Baby Sue in my aunt's basement?"

"I guess so. But I only read that in the papers. I never met Baby Sue."

"Let's go," Kushel said to Collier, handcuffing him.

"I always knew my brother would abandon me."

"Some brother," Kushel commented.

"Yes, he's a very strange person. I've known him all my life and I couldn't tell you what he would do from one moment to the next."

When Collier was safely in the van, Kushel took Rick aside.

"Rick, I'm going to have to talk to your aunt about all of this."

"I'm sure Aunt Mandy isn't involved. Maybe Collier's brother is this man in leather."

"Could be, but obviously this man has some connection to your aunt, and I have to find out what."

"I think Ice is our best bet."

"Yeah, I've thought of that. Why didn't she tell you about the Leather Man?"

"I don't know."

"Well, I'll put a tail on her. Look, Ricky, I know you like the girl but I've seen this kind of thing before. She may be more involved with this man than we know. But if she is, he's going to make a move soon. Meanwhile, when the media finds out about Felicia House, they'll be on your aunt's tail. You'd better warn her."

"Thanks, Kush," Rick said.

"And you'd better tell her that I want her to come down to the station house for questioning," Kushel added grimly.

31

Terrified, Ice lay on the floor. Above her, the Leather Man was running a snake whip over her body, from her toes to her neck.

"You're not scaring me," she said.

She knew he could tell she was lying for her naked body trembled, and she couldn't restrain her shivering movements.

The Leather Man had grabbed Ice as she walked on Broadway. It had been a simple operation. He'd stopped his van, jumped out and shoved her inside despite her attempts to protest. Ice hadn't been prepared because the Leather Man looked neuter in his new disguise. Only his skinhead made her apprehensive. But she'd been feeling very happy, and her reactions were dulled.

She knew they were somewhere in the Lower East Side in an abandoned building. She could see the padded walls and the chains on the boarded windows. If he were living here illegally, Ice knew there were no neighbors who might hear her scream.

He turned on a hot red light to spotlight her body.

"I hear you don't like snakes," he snarled.

She hated snakes more than anything on this earth.

"I'll do whatever you want but take that snake whip from my body," she argued quietly.

"Give me one good reason."

Oh, God, she thought, he's crazy.

"I won't hit you again, but you gotta do something for me."

"Anything," she promised.

When she saw the cuffs, Ice was startled. She resisted but quickly he put wrist cuffs and a neck cuff on her. The cuffs were connected to a chain in the Leather Man's hand. When he pulled the chain taut, Ice's body was tightened to a spreadeagle position.

Ice closed her eyes and murmured a prayer. Then, she sensed something. Her eyes flew open. Around the Leather Man, a green-gray snake wound its way from the floor to Leather Man's chest, its black and white patterns among the green-gray skin causing a strange jungle motif, as if large green foliage should surround it to make it real. Ice blinked her eyes. Was this an hallucination?

The snake was about ten feet long, and its head, with its strange cat's eyes, seemed to be examining Ice.

"This is Baby," Leather Man purred. "She's my best friend. When I got her, she was only two inches long. Look at how she's grown," he boasted with a weird crooning sound for his lullaby. "She's a python. Isn't she pretty?"

The snake moved from his body and began to search out Ice's perimeter, connecting her to the Leather Man with its long body.

"Tell me you don't like it and I'll stop it."

Ice began hyperventilating.

"Scream," he said.

Ice bit her lips blue.

"When it reaches you it's going to give you a big hug," he promised. "It may be your last, Ice."

"Don't," she begged.

"Uh, huh."

"Please," she pleaded.

He laughed. Then he threw down the chain that held her cuffs. She moved quickly away from the snake, causing the cuffs to break the skin on her wrists and blood began to rush to the bruised areas.

Ice felt sick. The snake was going to kill her.

"Please, take it away," she pleaded.

"Baby, Ice don't like you," the Leather Man crooned. "Why don't you give her a hug?"

Ice shook. The snake began winding down from the Leather Man's body, slithering toward her.

"Don't be mad, Baby. Ice will change her mind."

Ice propped her body against the wall. When the snake touched her, she screamed. The Leather Man laughed.

"Baby likes your screams, Ice. They turn her on. Now, she's going to give you that big hug I promised. She's going to hug those screams right out of you. You know what I mean? She's going to hug you to death, Ice."

Ice was at the point of lunacy. Good-bye, Ice, she thought.

"Baby loves you, Ice," he sangsong. "Who does Ice love?"

The snake began to move onto Ice's chest.

Suddenly, an unexpected creak in the floorboards caused the Leather Man to jump up. He poised, his whip ready to attack unwanted visitors.

The snake threw a loop around its prey, beginning the winding movements that would lead to Ice's suffocation.

Death, Ice thought, I'm beginning to respect you. I'm beginning to understand that you're the only thing everybody pays attention to. Be nice to me, Death. Please.

Then she heard Rick's voice. "It's the police," he shouted.

Through her blurry vision, Ice saw Rick and several policemen surround the Leather Man.

"Put down that whip," Kushel commanded.

The Leather Man turned, his eyes slanted with hate.

"You're too late," he hissed. "Ice will be dead in a minute."

The snake had wound its upper body around Ice's chest.

Each time she breathed, it constricted tighter, cutting off her oxygen. Ice was turning blue under its attack.

Quickly Rick looped its tail around his body and began uncoiling the snake in a backwards motion, causing its upper part to lose its grip on Ice.

"A knife," he shouted.

Kushel plunged into the Leather Man's S and M stash which held cuffs, whips, guns, and knives. He grabbed a long thick knife and gave it to Rick.

"You'll never do it," Leather Man boasted.

Rick waited until the snake's head left Ice's body and was on the floor, winding its way toward him. With a strong motion, Rick sliced its head off. The body continued to coil around Rick for a moment, then suddenly went limp. Rick grimaced as he untangled the deadly coils from his body. Then he faced the Leather Man.

"Give me the key," he demanded.

"Don't touch her," the Leather Man hissed. "She's mine."

"Slime," one cop muttered.

"Let's get her to a hospital. Forget the cuffs," Kushel said.

Rick picked Ice up into his arms.

"Read him his rights," Kushel instructed. "And handcuff him."

"Hey, Lieutenant, he's not a he," one cop said as he pulled at the Leather Man's skull. A plastic wig fell away and two long thick braids fell from a head of golden hair.

"A woman?" one cop whispered.

"Apparently," Kushel said grimly.

Then Kushel began peeling plastic from the Leather Man's face. Under the plastic was the wrinkled face of a demented woman.

"It's the Viking who attacked Rosie," Rick muttered.

"Who are you?" Kushel demanded.

"Ask Amanda Lord," was the hideous answer.

32

"So, *Amanda*, do you recognize me?" the tall muscular woman asked her visitor.

Dressed in blue prison uniform, her uniquely developed body conveyed the look of an Olympic champion, a Nietzschean superwoman. She laughed, her mouth revealing sharpened teeth. Her nostrils flared and above them, two deep blue eyes seemed like the eye of a hurricane, ready to attack at any provocation. Her thick blond-gray brows gave her the look of a scholar and a thinker. Above them, her forehead was high with many wrinkles. Her hair, pure blond from artificial coloring, was caught back severely at her temples and tightly woven into two thick long braids. She could be dressed for an appearance for a Wagnerian opera. All she needed was a shield and sword.

Amanda, sitting opposite the Viking, was an interesting contrast. Though both women were of the same age, Amanda's appearance conveyed a softness and elegance. Though her body also was strong and developed athletically, her surefootness was swift and positive, rather than the storm-trooper nature of her opponent. Amanda had dressed for this interview in a light gray chiffon suit. She wore elegant sandals, a matching gray bag and a straw hat; the outfit conveying the appearance of a middle-aged woman, happy with her life.

Now she strained to recognize the voice of the Viking.

"Have I met you before?" she asked.

Behind Amanda, Kushel and Rick watched the Viking.

"Amanda, do you mean I've changed that much?"

The Viking slurred her words in an European manner. Rick realized that Rosie had been right in her analysis that there was definitely a French influence to the Viking's speech. Yet her lips, thick and voluptuous, moved harshly in the motif of a Berlin film star.

"I don't think I know you," Amanda announced.

"Close your eyes and feel my energy," the Viking instructed.

Embarassed at this suggestion, Amanda turned to Rick with questions in her eyes.

"My aunt was good enough to appear here at your request," he said curtly. "Now, either reveal why you wanted to see her or we're leaving."

The Viking's mad eyes challenged Rick with consuming fury.

"You're her little darling nephew, aren't you?" She laughed loudly. "Her little Sonny."

"Come to the point," Kushel ordered brusquely.

"I never met you, Sonny, but I'm your godmother."

"My godmother is dead."

"Is she?" the Viking taunted.

Amanda gasped suddenly. Her eyes narrowed, examining this creature before her. She studied the Viking's stance, her eyes. Then she shook her head.

"Yes, Amanda," the Viking said. "I have changed, haven't I? The whole world turns against a beautiful woman when she has aged. Yes, Frau Amanda? You must know what it is to watch your magnificent body decay. Watching men look through you and wonder what you looked like when you were young. A woman of beauty who has been used to men at her beck and call and suddenly, there are no suitors. What can she do about it? Her flesh wrinkles. People wary of her needs. She must pay flunkies if she wants company. The young are bored with her. The old are boring to her. The young think she has a secret about life which they want to discover. If she becomes ill, the world ignores her. Yet, she has the appetites of a young woman. She still has passion. She still feels love, but there is no one to give it to.

"Do you know what it's like growing old? Yes, you must, Amanda. You must know."

"My God," Amanda turned white.

"Yes," the Viking lashed out savagely. "You finally know who I am, don't you, Amanda?"

"Yes . . ."

"Tell me, do I still have those fan clubs? Those cult clubs who watch my old films."

"I . . ."

"Yes, those cults think me a heroine. Those young studs who want to use me. The young girls who think they can replace me. No one can take my place," she lashed out, "I hate all young women."

Her face reddened with intense passion.

"Inside this aged body, I still feel. I still want. I react to men. But," her huge hands gripped the edge of her chair. "Men like young women. Well, they'll never take my place. I personally see to that. And you, Amanda, share some of the responsibility for this."

"What have I done?"

"Your energy kept drawing me to you. We were so very close that even when I died for the world's headlines and went through my transformation with sheep glands and various techniques to turn me into this superhuman woman, you had me still caught in your web. I followed you to this city. I ravaged my victims in your basement. I tortured them in the halfway house that you named after me. You wouldn't let me be, Amanda. You kept drawing me to you."

She rose with such force that the two police guards drew their weapons.

"Yes, Amanda, you share the responsibility for these murders. You gave me love and devotion. You were my only friend." The Viking's voice cracked. "And it was because of your love that I had to be near you."

Then she whirled about suddenly, kicking the two police guards into oblivion in one majestic movement. Kushel drew his gun but before he could fire, the Viking stomped him in the head, and he fell in a dead faint.

Rick was ready.

"So, my godson, it's you against me," the Viking taunted.

"You'll never leave here alive," Rick warned, watching her with concentrated energy.

"I don't want you to hurt him," Amanda said.

"I must be free to do my work," the Viking stated.

As she began her movement toward Rick, he felt the pit of his stomach turn into white fury. Then he folded his inner self into a metaphysical objective place, which his karate master had taught him, to defend himself against the Viking's pure superhuman energy.

Behind the Viking, Amanda grabbed the Viking's hands.

"Let me go. I don't want to hurt you," the Viking warned.

"You can't hurt me," Amanda said, holding her opponent firmly.

The superwoman turned, hesitating. Rick, taking advantage, karate-chopped her. The Viking hardly noticed.

"Amanda. Let my hands go," she ordered.

"I won't let you hurt Sonny."

The Viking merely shook Amanda from her. Amanda flew across the room, hitting her head as she slumped to the floor.

Rick, watching, rose to superhuman challenge. He kicked the Viking in the middle, then chopped her at the back of her neck, but these movements only stunned her. As she swung about to attack, Amanda called for help. Rick, blinded with concern for his aunt, turned and the Viking stomped him hard. The nerves of his body flooded with pain, sending messages to his central nervous system that if he continued, his systems would be demolished by his opponent's superior strength.

"Sonny," Amanda screamed.

The Viking turned away, stopped by the anguish in Amanda's voice. Rick jumped on the Viking's chest with all his strength. It was a lucky maneuver for her eyes filled with pain. He jumped on her chest again. Her wind began to go. She touched her chest in pain. Then she turned to Rick, her mouth opened with venom.

"You think you've won," she gasped.

Gnashing her teeth in a tormented crunching sound, her eyes seemed to turn inward as she let out a wail that chilled Rick to his soul. But, suddenly, she fell apart, reaching out toward him. Losing his apprehensive stance, Rick moved forward and she grabbed him around his throat, squeezing the very breath from his body. He prayed for strength but her hold on him was too great. Then, when he was ready to die, she lost her hold on him and fell to the floor.

Rick breathed several deep breaths. Then, regaining his composure, he raced over to his aunt.

"Are you okay?" he asked, helping Amanda to her feet.

"She could have killed me," Amanda said quietly. "But she didn't want to."

They walked over to the large body stretched out on the floor.

"She's dead, isn't she?" Amanda asked.

Rick traced the Viking's pulse, then shook his head.

"But how? I didn't hit her hard enough."

Rick pried open the Viking's mouth. He swore when he spotted an empty tooth which had probably held a poison capsule.

"Poison?" he commented.

"She did that once in a movie. She was playing the role

of an espionage agent. In the last scene, she bit into a poison capsule so that the secret police wouldn't get her to talk," Amanda said sadly.

"I'm sorry, Aunt Mandy," Rick said gently.

"Oh, Felicia," Amanda cried. "How could life have changed you so?"

33

Several weeks had passed during which Rosie had managed to write Chapters One through Five of the new book while recuperating from her bruises. When her doctors told her she was healed, she and Rick decided to throw a small party for Ice's new video, "Cling to Me," which had hit the charts. In a moment of extreme gratefulness, she'd invited her parents.

Now they surveyed the video crowd with disdain in their eyes.

"So," Mario said, "these are your friends? They're all strange."

Rosie laughed.

"Dad, this party is for Ice. They're important people in the video business. You know, MTM?"

"What's MTM?"

"It's the station with music," Celia said. "The one you think is filthy."

"Maybe we shouldn't have come to this party," Mario munched on a whitefish canapé and made a sour face. "Hey, what is this?"

"Relax, Dad."

"She's right, Mario," Rick agreed. "Hey, there's Kush."

Kushel and his wife, Drucila Kushel, both dressed in gray silk, were exiting from the elevator.

"That robot is scary," the detective said about Prince, who was handling the elevator.

"I never saw a robot pilot an elevator before," his wife agreed nervously.

"My wife, Drucila," Kushel introduced his petite mate proudly.

"Hello," Mario said, looking at Kushel with beady eyes to convey that he shouldn't get too friendly with Rosie and Rick.

"How's your aunt?" Kushel asked Rick.

"She's taking it badly. Felicia's memory was important to her. To find out your friend is a fiend is hard to take."

"Was she really your godmother?"

"Not formally. Aunt Mandy always said that she wanted that to happen but it never did."

"So who's your godmother?" Mario asked, examining the white linen suit Rick wore to match Rosie's white linen suit.

"Don't have one."

"That's terrible," Mario bellowed.

"Stop that. You're making Rick nervous," Rosie said.

She swung about in the chic white linen suit which sported short shorts instead of trousers. On her legs, she wore white mesh stockings dotted with pearl butterflies. White button-up shoes and white camellias in her hair completed her outfit. Matching his wife's, Rick's suit sported bermuda shorts and he wore a white safari hat with one camellia tucked into its brim.

Arm in arm, they smiled at their guests, busy tasting the shrimp, whitefish, and caviar canapés. At the dining room counter, herb tea and champagne were served below a large sign Rosie had printed that read: NO DRUGS ALLOWED.

"*SoHo Vice* is going to open next month," Rick told Mario proudly. "Want to come to the screening?"

"I thought those guys were wanted by the law," Mario said.

"Yes, but another studio is going to release it. Stu Vesco arranged it. He wants the picture released in time for the Academy Awards."

"So, who's that?" Mario pointed to the young girl at the center of the room.

"That's Ice," Rick explained.

"What kind of a name is that?"

"It's her professional name," Rosie laughed. "Want to meet her?"

"No."

"Dad, she's the guest of honor."

Rosie skipped over to Ice, who was the center of attention. Then, hand in hand, the two joined the family group.

Though Ice was also dressed in white, her dress was trashed, as usual. The skirt was torn into tiny threads escaping the hemline and covering her knees. The top was torn at the left shoulder, revealing a bra strap covered with rhinestones. Her puppetlike makeup and her closely cropped hair highlighted the long rhinestone earrings she wore. She was barefoot and on her toes rhinestone rings shone.

Celia stared at Ice, shaking her head at her outfit.

"This is Ice," Rosie introduced. "You know Detective Kushel. This is his wife, Drucila. And my mom and dad."

"Hi," Ice said nervously.

"What kind of a name is Ice?" Mario demanded.

"It's my stage name."

"What's your real name?"

"It's Bonni," she revealed.

"I like that," Mario stated. Then gallantly he took Ice's hand and kissed it.

"I wish you good luck and success," he said sweetly. Then to his wife, "Celia, let's go. This party is for young people. Kushel, can I give you a lift?"

Kushel laughed anxiously.

"Come on, Detective. We'll have supper."

Kushel looked at Rick.

"Can I trust him?" he asked.

"Kush. Mario will show you a great time. He's a wonderful host," Rick laughed.

In the elevator, Celia rubbed Mario's lips with her clean handkerchief, warning him that he might have caught a disease by kissing that strange girl's hand.

Back at the party, Ice thanked Rick and Rosie for the festivities.

"Neat," Rosie said.

"I'm glad you're not mad because I didn't tell you who that awful man was. I wanted to protect you. I never thought there was a connection between him and that woman who attacked you," Ice explained.

"We understand," Rick said, putting his arm around Rosie. "Hey, sweetheart, how about a dance?"

As they floated about the floor, Rick whispered, "You know, Mrs. Ramsey, I continue to adore you."

"Mr. Ramsey, keep saying things like that and you'll never be single again."

"Hopefully," he laughed.

"Hey, I've got an idea."

"Yes?"

"When the party's over we'll get into bed and . . ."

"Yes?"

"Write Chapter Six."

"Oh, Rosie."

"Come on. It'll be fun."

"Promise."

"We'll take breaks."

"Sounds swell."